# DEADLY DRIVER

A staccato burst of sharp explosions ripped through the air, and Amanda shrieked. Without thinking she threw herself into Mick's arms. "That sounded like gunshots!"

"Relax." Mick folded his arms around her protectively. "It's just fireworks. Today's the first day of the Chinese New Year."

"I guess I'm a little jumpy," Amanda confessed as she slid into the passenger seat of the car. "None of what's happened to Pepper's photos makes any sense."

Mick settled in the driver's seat and started the engine. They pulled out of the parking lot and headed for Fleet Street. Just after they crossed the intersection a white van appeared in the lane ahead of them. Amanda realized with horror that it was headed the wrong way.

"Look out!" she cried. "It's in our lane."

Mick hit the horn . . . but the van kept coming.

Other Bantam Books you will enjoy
Ask your bookseller for the books you have missed

AMONG FRIENDS by Caroline B. Cooney

AN ALMOST PERFECT SUMMER by Rona S. Zable

CAMP GIRL-MEETS-BOY by Caroline B. Cooney

CREDIT-CARD CAROLE by Sheila Solomon Klass

DOUBLE JEOPARDY (Sweet Valley High Super Thriller #2) created by Francine Pascal

ON DANGEROUS GROUND (Private Eyes #3) by Julia Winfield

A FAMILY APART (Book 1 in the Orphan Train Quartet) by Joan Lowery Nixon

THE PERFECT GUY by Ann Herrick

EVVIE AT SIXTEEN by Susan Beth Pfeffer

WATCHER IN THE MIST by Norma Johnston

WHISPER OF THE CAT by Norma Johnston

HART AND SOUL #4

# *GET THE PICTURE*

### JAHNNA N. MALCOLM

BANTAM BOOKS

NEW YORK • TORONTO • LONDON • SYDNEY • AUCKLAND

*RL 6, age 12 and up*

*GET THE PICTURE*
*A Bantam Book / August 1990*

ISBN 0-553-28191-7

*Published simultaneously in the United States and Canada*

Bantam Books are published by Bantam Books, a division of Bantam Doubleday Dell Publishing Group, Inc. Its trademark, consisting of the words "Bantam Books" and the portrayal of a rooster, is Registered in U.S. Patent and Trademark Office and in other countries. Marca Registrada. Bantam Books, 666 Fifth Avenue, New York, New York 10103.

PRINTED IN THE UNITED STATES OF AMERICA

O     0 9 8 7 6 5 4 3 2 1

*For Jim Walcott-Ayers,*
*friend for life*

# CHAPTER ONE

*I*t's gone!"

Pepper Larson's stunned voice echoed around the vast rotunda of San Francisco's City Hall. She stared at the blank space on the wall where her photo exhibit should have been hanging. That morning she had personally mounted her ten pictures in that spot, and now they were missing.

Being chosen as one of the four teen finalists in San Francisco's Picture the City photography contest was the best thing that had ever happened to the redheaded junior. Pepper, who was not usually a clothes horse, had even bought a green velvet pantsuit with a white silk blouse and black patent leather loafers in honor of the official opening that afternoon.

She looked around miserably at the crowd that was gathering for the exhibition and groaned. The biggest moment of her life had just become the biggest disaster.

"Help!" Pepper shouted. "I've been robbed!"

A woman in a pale gray suit carrying a clipboard hurried across the marble floor of the

1

courthouse. She wore a name tag that read, "Hello, I'm Kate Brehony."

"Shhh!" The woman placed a long painted fingernail to her lips. "Your voice really carries in here."

"Good!" Pepper shoved her wire-rimmed glasses up on her nose. "I *want* to be heard."

The woman put her hand on Pepper's elbow and escorted her over to the wall. "Now, what seems to be the problem?"

"My photos—I mean, my exhibit." Pepper gestured wildly at the blank wall. "It was supposed to be right there, and it's gone! I can't believe it." Pepper fell back against one of the marble pillars and ran her hands through her curly red hair.

"Maybe it hasn't been hung yet," Mrs. Brehony suggested.

Pepper shook her head. "It was here. I hung it myself this morning. Someone has stolen it." Hot tears sprang to her eyes. "Why? Why would someone do that?"

"Now, let's not jump to hasty conclusions," the lady said, dropping her voice to an exaggerated whisper. "There's probably a perfectly logical explanation."

"I thought you guys were supposed to watch out for our work." Pepper paced back and forth in front of her exhibition spot. "Who's in charge here, anyway?"

A number of people had already arrived for the opening of the exhibition. They stared curiously in Pepper's direction as her voice grew louder and louder.

"I'm just hosting the opening reception," Mrs. Brehony replied. "But there are other people in charge of the security arrangements."

"Well, they haven't done a very good job," Pepper said, raising her voice indignantly. "I mean, there are only four of us. How hard is it to keep an eye on four photo displays?"

Looking back at the exhibition, Pepper noticed a rotund young man standing proudly beside a series of photographic portraits. An older couple who were almost as immense stood beside him.

"Are you one of the finalists?" Pepper demanded, as she marched up beside them.

The boy shot her a startled look, then nodded. "Yes, I'm Richard Reely. Are you—?"

"Did you see anyone messing with my entry?" Pepper interrupted.

"Sorry?"

"My entry." Pepper gestured at the blank wall. "It's gone. Did you see anyone tampering with it?"

"No," the boy replied. "We only got here a few minutes ago."

"Well, someone's stolen it," Pepper declared, "and I want to know who." She ran frantically over to the exhibit on the other side of where hers should have been. There was a name card above the photographs that read, "Children of the City, by Susan Wan," but there was no sign of the photographer.

Pepper hurried on to the last display, where a scrawny teen with huge horn-rimmed glasses stood admiring the prints on the panel. As Pepper came up beside him, he announced, "Pretty impressive, aren't they?"

"I wouldn't know," Pepper said in irritation. She started to leave. "I thought you were the photographer."

The boy smiled proudly. "I am."

Pepper narrowed her eyes suspiciously. "Martin Watts?"

The boy nodded in acknowledgment.

"You didn't see anyone take my entry, did you?"

"What entry?" the boy shot back. "Who are you, anyway?"

"I'm Pepper Larson." She turned and shouted to the room, "I'm a finalist, and someone's stolen my entry."

Richard Reely joined them, followed by an anxious Mrs. Brehony. "Why would anyone want to steal photographs?" the heavyset boy asked. "Are you sure you haven't just lost them?"

"No way!"

"Why would anyone want to steal *your* work?" Martin Watts asked smugly. "I'll bet you got cold feet, once you got a good look at the competition."

"What!" Pepper shouted.

"Please, keep your voice down! I'm sorry,

everyone, we will handle this quietly." Mrs. Brehony took Pepper firmly by the elbow and led her away from the others. She flipped nervously through the pages on her clipboard. "Now, what was the name of your entry?"

"Graffiti as Art," Pepper said, pointing over the woman's shoulder to the line where her name appeared on the list. "I should retitle it San Francisco Crime Victim, Number Three Million."

"Oh, dear, this just won't do," Mrs. Brehony muttered, looking as though the gravity of the situation was starting to sink in. "I mean, this *is* City Hall . . ."

Pepper put her hands on her hips. "Look, are you going to call the police, or should I?"

"Police?" the woman gasped. "Now, don't be hasty. There must be some other explanation. We don't want to alarm all of our guests unnecessarily."

"Guests!" Pepper had forgotten all about them. She had invited her aunt and uncle from San Mateo. They would be arriving with her mother. And her best friend, Amanda Hart, was supposed to join her for the reception. Of course, they would understand. But what about her friends from Sutter Academy—especially handsome Peter Yang, president of the senior class?

Pepper stared down at her brand-new outfit and her chin started to quiver. "I went to all this trouble to get dressed up for nothing."

"Please, Miss Larson," Mrs. Brehony hissed. "Try to get a grip on yourself."

A sickening feeling suddenly swept over Pepper. *What if the judges changed their minds about me?* she thought. *What if I'm not really one of the finalists?*

"Peter's going to—they're *all* going to think I was disqualified from the competition," Pepper groaned. "I'll die of embarrassment."

"I wouldn't worry—"

"I have to make some phone calls," Pepper interrupted the woman. "I'll be right back."

Pepper raced for the lobby and the telephone booths. She had to call her friends and tell them not to come. Then she would wait for Amanda to get there.

"Mandy will know what to do," Pepper muttered under her breath. "I hope."

# CHAPTER TWO

A manda Hart hurried down the street to City Hall. The chilly wind whipped through her long dark hair, and she pulled her full-length black wool coat tighter around her. Amanda couldn't help smiling. She had spent almost a week searching for the perfect gift for her friend Pepper. And she had finally found it. It had been hanging right on her bedroom wall the whole time.

She made sure she had a tight grip on the bag that contained the framed and signed photograph her parents had taken while on assignment in Belfast. That photo had won them the Pulitzer Prize five years before. Amanda only wished they could be there in person to give it to Pepper.

She squeezed her eyes closed as she tried to remember where her parents were this week. As famous photojournalists, they were constantly on the move. The week before they had called her from Afghanistan. Before that she had gotten a call from a ship in the Persian Gulf.

When she reached City Hall, Amanda spotted

a familiar head of curly red hair at the top of the steps. Pepper waved frantically, and Amanda could tell by the look on her friend's face that something was wrong. She hurried up the steps. "Pepper, what's the matter?"

"The most awful thing has happened," Pepper wailed. "My entry's gone!"

She led Amanda quickly to the place where her entry should have been. "The worst thing is that no one around here seems upset about it except me. They think it's just a mix-up."

"Have you told the police?" Amanda asked.

Pepper shook her head. "I'm afraid to. I had this horrible idea that maybe the committee disqualified me from the finals at the last minute and never told me." She shuddered at the thought.

"Now, don't get paranoid," Amanda said soothingly. "I'm sure there's a logical explanation."

"Well, just in case, I've called everyone I could and told them not to come."

Amanda handed Pepper the brightly colored little bag she held in her hand. "In the meantime, here's a little present. I hope it will make you feel better."

"A present?" Pepper looked in the bag, and her eyes immediately filled with tears. "Oh, Mandy!"

Amanda snapped her fingers and then dug in her coat pocket. "And this is from my aunt and uncle and cousin Josh. They gave it to me just before they left."

"They're out of town?"

Amanda nodded. "They had to go to Aunt Jane's library conference in Hawaii, remember?"

"Must be rough," Pepper cracked.

"It's just for four days, but they wanted to make sure you got this." Amanda handed Pepper a pale blue envelope. Because her parents were on the road so much, Amanda lived with her aunt and uncle, Jane and Silas Pickering. Her parents felt it was important that she finish high school in one place.

Pepper tore open the envelope and then grinned at the card inside. "That's so sweet."

A low murmur signaled that a crowd had begun to gather for the exhibit. Each guest had been given a program with brief descriptions of the entries and their photographers. In the center of the crowd was a white-haired woman in a gray suit clutching a clipboard. A smile was plastered on her face as she strode purposely toward the girls.

"Who's that?" Amanda whispered to Pepper.

"That's Mrs. Brehony." Pepper shoved her glasses up on her nose. "She's in charge of this fiasco."

When the lady reached them, she immediately dropped her smile and spoke in a hoarse whisper. "I talked to our security people, and they suggested a possible explanation for your missing entry. There was another exhibit in the rotunda that was taken down this morning. They think perhaps your photos were packed and put on the truck by mistake."

Pepper shrugged. "Then we can just get them off the truck."

The woman patted her hair nervously with one hand. "That's impossible. You see, that truck is on its way to New York."

"What!" Pepper shrieked.

"Take it easy, Pep," Amanda said, squeezing her friend's arm. She turned to the woman and asked calmly, "Can't you call the driver and tell him to stop?"

The woman looked at Amanda in confusion. "I'm sorry, I don't believe we've met. Do you have something to do with this exhibit?"

Amanda pulled out her student press card from her school and declared, "Amanda Hart, editor-in-chief of the *Sutter Spectator*. We sponsored Pepper's entry."

"I see." The woman tucked the clipboard under her arm. "Well, we will try to reach the driver this evening."

"But what am I supposed to do?" Pepper wailed. "The judging is in less than a week."

"This is all so unfortunate." Mrs. Brehony glanced uneasily at the crowd gathering around them. "The only thing I can suggest is that you try to reconstruct your photo essay, just in case we can't get hold of the driver, or in the event the entry isn't on the truck."

"What?" Pepper gasped. "Do you know how

long it took me to develop and mount those pictures? Hours. Days. I'll never get it done in time."

Mrs. Brehony shrugged helplessly. "I don't know what else you can do." She put one hand on Pepper's arm. "I promise to make sure the judges take all that's happened into consideration when they judge the competition."

"Mrs. Brehony!" a man called from across the room. "We need you at the reception table."

"Excuse me, I must go. But I promise to call you the minute I know anything." A look of relief covered the woman's face as she walked quickly away.

"Can you believe that?" Pepper exclaimed. "This project took me all semester, and she thinks I can whip it together—like *that*!" She snapped her fingers.

"Now, don't get so upset," Amanda replied. "Where are your negatives?"

"In the Coop back at Sutter." Pepper blew her bangs off her forehead with a rush of breath. "I guess I'll have to go back and start over."

"Am I too late?" a voice called from behind Amanda's shoulder. "The line for the parking garage was so slow, I thought I'd never get here."

"Peter!" Amanda exclaimed, as she turned to face the slender, dark-haired boy. He was dressed in gray wool slacks and a blue blazer and looked every inch the school leader that he was. "The reception is just starting."

"Great." Peter Yang nodded at Amanda and then turned his smile on Pepper. "Hi, Pepper. You look fantastic."

Pepper stared up at the handsome boy with a dazed expression on her face. Without thinking she reached up and removed the wire-rimmed glasses perched on her nose.

"Uh, Pepper?" Amanda gently nudged her friend. "Peter was saying . . ."

"Oh, gosh, I'm sorry." Pepper shook her head and giggled with embarrassment. "It's just that . . . well, when I asked you to come to the reception, I didn't really think you'd come. I mean, after all, you're pretty busy with the senior class, and I'm just a lowly junior." Her eyes widened and she sputtered, "What I mean is—"

"Pepper's a little upset," Amanda cut in hurriedly. "You see, her exhibit is missing."

"It may have been stolen," Pepper added dramatically.

The smile vanished from Peter's face. "That's terrible. What can we do?"

"Well, at this point, nothing," Amanda replied. "The lady in charge thinks it may have disappeared with the last exhibit."

"Which is pretty hard to believe," Pepper said, recovering her cool. "The last exhibit was oil paintings. You'd have to be pretty dim to confuse

black-and-white   photographs   with   full-color
paintings."

"So what can you do?" Peter asked.

Pepper sighed. "Start over."

"Do you have the negatives?"

"They're back at school." Amanda turned to
Pepper. "Do you have your car?"

"No. I took the bus."

Peter took his hands out of his pockets. "Look,
I'll drive you there."

Pepper's eyes lit up, but she said, "Oh, Peter,
that's such a pain. Are you sure?" Before Peter
could answer, she blurted, "I'll get my purse."

Peter smiled. "And if I can get my car back
from the garage, I'll meet you two out front."

"It's a deal," Amanda said.

Pepper watched the dapper senior jog toward
the front entrance of City Hall and sighed. "Isn't
he handsome? I can't believe he actually came to
see me." She threw her hands up in the air in
disgust. "And I can't believe I acted like such a
geek."

"Well, except for the lowly junior stuff, you
were just fine." Amanda nudged Pepper. "Hurry
and get your purse. We don't want to keep him
waiting."

Pepper scurried to the cloakroom, where she
had checked her purse and her 35mm camera.
She looped the purse over her shoulder and the
Nikon around her neck, then joined Amanda.
"Let's go."

There was a sudden flurry of movement by the entrance to the main corridor. A battery of television cameramen and photographers burst through the door, then turned and trained their lenses back at the entrance.

At least a dozen heavily armed sheriff's deputies hustled a middle-aged Asian man into the building. He was elegantly dressed in a pale beige double-breasted silk suit. All at once the reporters began shouting questions at the prisoner, who remained impassively silent.

"What's going on?" Pepper murmured to Amanda, who shook her head.

"Let's find out." Amanda moved closer and collided with a beefy man carrying a thick sheaf of papers. The papers scattered all over the floor, and Amanda quickly knelt down to help pick them up. "I'm sorry. I didn't see you."

"Forget it," the man replied brusquely. Something about him seemed familiar to Amanda. He was about thirty, with thinning hair and a thick moustache.

"You're Sergeant Rubano, aren't you?" she declared suddenly.

The man gave her a surprised look. "Right."

"I knew I'd seen you before," Amanda said. "You came to Sutter Academy a few months ago and gave an assembly. Part of the Task Force Against Drugs."

"Right again."

"Your business suit threw me," Amanda said.

"When you gave your talk, you were wearing a '49ers jersey and a pair of old jeans."

The policeman looked impressed. "You've got a good memory." Then he glanced at his plain brown suit and grimaced. "I hate these monkey suits. Only wear them when I have to appear in court."

"Is that what the commotion's all about?"

He nodded and glanced at his watch. "Listen, I'd like to talk, but I've got to get to the court-room.

"What's going on?" Pepper asked.

Sergeant Rubano shook the sheaf of papers in his hand. "Ever hear of Willie 'the Chairman' Chow?"

"He's a gang leader, isn't he?" Amanda replied.

"Right. In Chinatown."

"Was that him?" Pepper asked, wide-eyed. "Wow! I've never seen a gangster before."

"The Chairman's one of the worst this town's ever seen," the sergeant said. "Probably behind half the crack coming into this city. And abso-lutely ruthless."

"I read he was arrested for murdering a China-town businessman," Amanda said.

"Yeah, the trial starts today. We've got a witness who can connect Willie directly to the hit."

"It really is a stroke of luck running into you," Amanda said, "because we were just looking for a policeman."

Sergeant Rubano raised his eyebrows. "What's the matter?" They hurriedly filled him in on the missing exhibit.

"That's too bad." The detective glanced once again in the direction of the courtroom. "Look, I'm sorry, kids, but I've got to get back to work. Talk to the cops down at the precinct headquarters. If they can't help you . . ." He reached into his pocket and pulled out a card. "Give me a call."

"Well, he was a big help," Pepper grumbled, as she watched the policeman disappear down the corridor.

Amanda smiled at her friend. "Forget about him. We've got more important things to do."

"Yeah." Pepper giggled, as they watched Peter Yang pull his silver sports car up in front of the building. "Like ride in Peter's new car."

By the time they turned into the parking lot at Sutter Academy, Pepper had worked up a good head of steam over the exhibit. "I mean, you wouldn't believe that jerk Martin Watts, acting like I couldn't take the competition. Who does he think he is, anyway?" She snorted derisively. "I saw his pictures. They're all of little bird's nests."

"Where should I drop you off?" Peter interrupted gently.

"Over by the Coop." Amanda pointed to the old carriage house at the far end of the campus that served as the Journalism classroom. At one time chickens had been kept there, which was how the cottage got its nickname.

He pulled to a stop by the curb, and Amanda and Pepper quickly thanked him and hopped out of the car. Peter smiled and waved, then gunned the motor as he pulled away from the curb.

Amanda led Pepper down the walkway, rummaging through her purse for her keys. When she was a few feet from the cottage she heard Pepper gasp.

"What is it?" Amanda asked, turning to look at her friend.

"Look at the Coop." Pepper pointed to the smashed window of the little cottage. Glass was everywhere, and the door was wide open.

Amanda gripped Pepper's arm. "Oh, no!"

# CHAPTER THREE

T his place is a disaster area!"

Amanda stared at the ruined office in complete shock. The long tables used for layout and paste-up were turned over on their sides. The supply cabinet had been completely ransacked, and pens, paper clips, and other office supplies were spilled across the floor. The filing cabinets were tipped over, and back issues of the *Sutter Spectator* lay strewn across the room.

"Mr. Mooney's desk has been totaled," Pepper exclaimed as she stepped gingerly over to their faculty advisor's green metal desk. Every drawer had been yanked out and emptied onto the ground.

"This'll take days to clean up." Amanda felt her temper rise. "If I ever find out who did this, I'll—I'll . . ." She clenched her fists helplessly.

"Some people are really sick!" Pepper muttered as she stared at the wreckage.

Amanda noticed some floppy disks lying on the floor beside the desk and gasped. "Oh, no, not the computer!" She raced over to the corner where their PC was placed and heaved a quick sigh of relief. "At least they didn't touch it."

Pepper scratched her head. "That's the most valuable thing in the room. If they were going to steal something, that should have been it."

"Looks like they didn't want to steal, they just wanted to destroy." Amanda kicked at the debris on the floor. "Ooh, this makes me mad."

"I'm just glad we got this week's issue to the printer," Pepper said, putting the drawers back in Mr. Mooney's desk. "At least we won't have to do that all over again."

"I'm calling the police," Amanda declared. She rummaged through the papers around Mr. Mooney's desk for the phone.

"I'd better see what else got hit." Pepper disappeared into the back room.

"Why'd these vandals have to trash the Coop?" Amanda shouted to Pepper as she picked up a handful of newspapers and slammed them down on the desk. "I mean, okay, something like this happens to the school about once a year. Usually someone paints dirty words on the gym, or something stupid like that." Amanda finally uncovered the phone and, picking up the receiver, punched in the number for the police station. "But why *my* newspaper? I don't understand!"

"I think I do."

Pepper's voice was a dull monotone. She walked stiffly back into the main room. "Check out the darkroom. My negatives are gone."

"What!" Amanda hung up the phone and ran to the door of the little utility closet that had been converted into a darkroom.

"Someone stole my pictures from the exhibit," Pepper muttered under her breath. "And now they've tried to sabotage any chance I have of winning the competition by stealing my negatives."

"Pepper, I know you're upset," Amanda said gently, "but don't you think you're exaggerating a little here? This is just a case of vandalism."

"How can you say that?" Pepper replied. "I had the negative file on the shelf, right in plain sight, and it's gone."

"Come on, Pepper," Amanda said, losing her patience. "Why would someone go to these lengths to keep you out of a dumb contest?"

"Gee, thanks, Amanda," Pepper said sarcastically. "I really appreciate your support."

"Well, you're not the only victim here," Amanda shot back. "This newspaper is my life."

Pepper put her hands on her hips. "Oh, yeah? Well, the photo competition is the most important thing that has ever happened to me."

Amanda tossed her hair over her shoulder and glared at Pepper. "If this contest was so important to you, why did you leave your negatives lying around like that?"

"I didn't just leave them lying around," Pepper sputtered. "In fact, I put them in a special place . . ." Pepper's voice drifted off, and suddenly she spun and raced back into the darkroom.

"What are you doing?" Amanda asked, hurrying after her.

Pepper was on her knees in front of the cabinet beneath the sink. "I just remembered, I hid them," she said excitedly. Pepper felt around inside the metal cabinet and removed a long, thin pencil box. "Thank God, they're here!"

Amanda and Pepper completely forgot about their argument and hugged each other tightly. Then Pepper led the way to the one standing table by the computer and cleared off a spot.

"I wanted to keep these negatives separate from the newspaper's stuff," she explained as she set the pencil box on the table. "So at the last minute I stored them in here." Pepper carefully opened the lid and held the negatives up to the light one by one.

"There are only nine negatives, Pepper," Amanda said, looking over her shoulder. "I thought you had ten pictures in the exhibit."

"I did." Pepper looked confused, then hit her head with her hand. "Now I remember. I didn't like the way one of the prints turned out, so I did it over again." She took off her glasses and rubbed her eyes. "I must have just tucked that last negative into the open file . . ."

"Are you sure?" Amanda asked.

"I think so." Pepper slipped her glasses back on her nose. "But that was weeks ago. It's hard to be certain."

"Do you have any other copies of the tenth picture?" Amanda asked.

Pepper bit her lip. "I left some contact sheets back at my house. There might be an early proof with them. I could make another negative from that." She grimaced. "But it'd never look right."

"Is there any alternative?" Amanda said.

Pepper shook her head. "We'd better go see if it's there." She got up and looked around the debris-strewn room. "Should we clean up this mess first?"

Amanda shook her head. "It's Friday. We have all weekend to fix the Coop. I'll call Mr. Mooney right now and tell him about it. Then we'll just lock the door and put something over the window."

While Amanda dialed their teacher, Pepper found a piece of wood in one of the closets and a hammer in Mr. Mooney's desk. "Look," she cried with glee. "He even has nails." She held up three rusted objects. "At least, I think these are nails."

When Pepper had finished pounding the board into place over the broken window, Amanda patted her on the back. "Good work. Now, if we hurry, we can just catch the next bus to your house."

The bus was easing up the the curb when the girls reached the stop. They slipped into a seat at the back and rehashed the events of the day.

Finally Amanda said, "Look, Pepper, I'm sorry

I lost my temper back there. I was just a little upset about what happened to the Coop."

Pepper lowered her glasses to peer comically at her friend. "Well, I didn't exactly keep a cool head either."

"We've probably made a big fuss over nothing." Amanda leaned back in her seat and giggled. "By the time we get to your house, Mrs. Brehony will have phoned—"

"To say the truck driver brought the pictures back and wants to beg my forgiveness," Pepper finished for her.

"And the judges were so impressed that they decided to give you the medal now."

Pepper clapped her hands together. "And Martin Watts will have been disqualified from the contest for being such a boring geek."

When they reached Pepper's street, she pulled the buzzer, and the two hopped onto the sidewalk as the bus came to a halt. In spite of all that had happened that day, they were feeling light-hearted as they headed toward Pepper's house. But something down the street stopped them both in their tracks.

Blue lights from a patrol car were flashing in front of a white stucco house with a red tiled roof.

"Pepper," Amanda whispered. "That's your house!"

# CHAPTER FOUR

The two girls ran full speed down the street just as another police car pulled to a stop in front of the Larson home.

"What's happened?" Pepper yelled as the officer got out of the car. "Is my mom all right?"

"She's fine," a policewoman called from the front porch. "She's on the phone with your father. But there's been a break-in here." She directed her words at the new officer, who trotted up to join her. "A forcible entry through the back door, but, surprisingly, not much was taken. It's a little odd."

Pepper raced up the steps, with Amanda close behind her. The Larsons' home was ultramodern, with glass and chrome architecture. Mrs. Larson worked as an interior decorator, and the place reflected her taste in modern art. The living room had soaring cathedral ceilings with dramatic skylights showering the paintings on the walls with natural light. The canvases were mostly great splashes of primary color that stood out in vivid relief against the white couches and carpet.

"The living room was untouched," the police-woman, whose badge read "K. Schneider," informed them. She led the other officer and the girls into the dining room. "But the drawers of the sideboard have been emptied."

"Looks like they were searching for something in particular," the policeman remarked. "Silver?"

"Naw. That's all still here," the woman answered. "But one of the upstairs rooms has been searched from top to bottom."

Pepper looked at Amanda and groaned. "I think I know which room it is."

She took the carpeted steps two at a time and raced down the hall to her second-floor bedroom. When Amanda reached the door, Pepper murmured, "*Now* do you think it's just a coincidence?"

Amanda stepped through the door and gasped. Everything in Pepper's room had been turned upside down. The mattress had been pulled off the box spring and torn open. Wads of stuffing littered the floor. Worst of all, the photographs Pepper had taken over the years had been ripped off the wall and pulled out of their frames. Shards of glass crackled under their feet. Every drawer had been ransacked, and the shoe boxes from the shelf in her closet covered the floor.

"Look, my photo albums have been torn apart." She slumped onto the creaking box spring of her bed. "Why are they doing this to me? What do they want?"

"Honey, this is terrible." Mrs. Larson stood in the doorway. She had red hair and dark eyes, just like her daughter, but her luminous skin and regal features gave her a sophisticated bearing that Pepper could never imitate. From her father Pepper had inherited her freckles and turned-up nose, along with her nearsightedness.

Mrs. Larson nodded hello to Amanda, then gingerly sat down beside her daughter on the bed.

"You must feel just awful," she said, hugging Pepper close.

"Mom," Pepper hissed. "They're after me!"

"Now you mustn't take this personally," Mrs. Larson said. "Unfortunately, these kinds of robberies happen all the time. Officer Schneider thinks that I probably came home while they were just getting started and scared them away."

"Either that, or they left because they couldn't find what they wanted," Amanda said, looking meaningfully into Pepper's eyes.

"Well, I'm just relieved that they didn't get the Jasper Johns painting in the living room." Mrs. Larson attempted a smile. "Fortunately for us, they weren't connoisseurs of art."

The policewoman appeared at the door with a clipboard. "Mrs. Larson?"

"Yes, Officer Schneider?"

"Officer Hamma and I would like you to make a list of what's missing for our report." The two police officers stepped gingerly into the room.

"This is just so distressing, I . . . I can hardly

think." Mrs. Larson pressed her hand to her forehead in concentration. "They don't seem to have taken anything of value. I think my jewelry is all there, but I'll have to look more closely."

"I'm missing something," Pepper declared, standing up. "My red photo album with all the pictures I've taken since the sixth grade."

"Oh, honey, please be serious."

"I am!" Pepper protested. "That album documents my growth as a photographer. It's very valuable to me."

The officers exchanged looks but didn't write anything down. Pepper picked up one of the drawers from her dressing table and said, "It looks like my Instamatic camera is missing, too."

"You still have that?" her mother asked. "Why, when we got you such a nice professional camera?"

"I keep it for sentimental reasons," Pepper muttered. "But that's beside the point. I'm telling them what's missing, and they aren't writing any of it down." She turned and glared at the officers. "What's the matter—don't you believe me?"

"Sure," Officer Hamma said patiently, "but it's hard to believe someone would break into a house just to steal an old camera and a photo album."

"Pepper, where is your new camera?" Mrs. Larson asked.

"Right here." She pulled it out of her purse, and Mrs. Larson scooped it out of her hands. "What are you doing?"

"I want to put this in your father's safe in his study," Mrs. Larson said. "Just in case these thieves come back."

Pepper opened her mouth in outrage, and Amanda quickly stepped forward. "Mrs. Larson, we have reason to believe that someone is after the pictures Pepper shot for the photo contest, not her camera."

"Photo contest?" the policewoman asked.

"Yes, the Picture the City competition. It's a *very* big deal!" Pepper's voice quivered with indignation. "And I'm a finalist."

"Honey, I know you're upset," Mrs. Larson said soothingly, "but that's no reason to raise your voice—"

Pepper spun to face her mother. "Maybe if I shout, they'll listen to me!"

"Her photo essay was stolen right out of City Hall," Amanda added.

"Did you report it?" Officer Schneider asked.

"No, but that was because at the time we weren't sure it was stolen." Amanda realized the moment she said the words that the police weren't going to believe her. "But we did talk to Sergeant Rubano about it."

This seemed to catch their interest. "What did he say?" Officer Hamma asked.

"Not much," Pepper admitted. "He was in a hurry."

Officer Schneider tucked the clipboard under her arm. "Mrs. Larson, I'm sure your daughter has had something taken from her, and, of course, she's understandably distressed about it."

"But there's been a rash of break-ins in this neighborhood," the other officer cut in, "and we've been stepping up our patrols."

Mrs. Larson smoothed her neatly coiffed hair lightly with her palm. "I've told my husband time and time again that we need an alarm system. Maybe this will convince him."

"That's a good idea." He gestured for her to follow him out into the hall. "Until you get one, I can point out a few extra precautions you might take."

"Thank you." As Mrs. Larson followed the officers down the hall to the stairs, the girls heard Pepper's mother say, "Please don't mind my daughter. She has an excitable nature . . ."

"I don't believe it," Amanda exclaimed angrily. "How can they be so casual about it?"

Pepper shook her head in frustration. "Just because I'm a teenager, they won't listen to me."

"That's infuriating!" Amanda leaped to her feet. "There ought to be somebody we can write or call."

"Who're we going to call?" Pepper said sarcastically. "The police?"

"Your life is in danger, and they ignore you!" Amanda shook her fist at the hallway.

"Hold it! Time out!" Pepper held up one hand. "Did you say my life is in danger?"

Amanda nodded.

"*Now* who's jumping to conclusions?" Pepper crossed her arms in front of her.

Amanda dug in her purse for her ballpoint pen and lavender notepad. She always thought better with a pen in her hand. "Look, whoever's doing this knows where you live. They didn't find what they wanted here or at the Coop, so the next thing they'll probably do is come for you."

"Why?"

"To see if you're carrying the negatives with you, in your purse, or something."

Pepper's face turned ghostly white. "Mandy, are you sure?"

"Of course not. But I don't think you should stay here tonight. Not after this."

"Where am I going to stay?"

"I'd say my house," Amanda said, nibbling on one fingernail. "But since they knew about the Coop and your house, they probably know where I live, too."

Pepper nodded. "Besides, that would be too scary, being there all by ourselves."

"I've got it!" Amanda snapped her fingers. "It will take some fast talking, but I think it would be the perfect place for us to hide."

"Where?"

Amanda wrote the words on her pad. "Fleet Street."

"Are you out of your mind?" Pepper shrieked.

Fleet Street was the bicycle messenger service

owned and run by their friends Mickey Soul and Gabriel Sanchez.

"Mick has helped us so many times before, I'm sure he'll think it's a good idea."

As Amanda talked, she absentmindedly drew his face on the notepad. The strong jaw with a tiny cleft in the chin. A shock of dark hair falling lazily on the forehead. But it was his eyes— piercing and blue—that she remembered the most. Amanda looked down at her sketch and smiled.

"I don't doubt Mick would go for it," Pepper declared with a smirk. "It's my mother I'm worried about. She'd absolutely hate the idea."

"Shhh! She might hear you." Amanda closed the door of Pepper's bedroom. As she did, she could hear the sound of a phone ringing downstairs.

"Besides, what would I tell her?" Pepper put on her sweetest voice. "Oh, by the way, Mom, I won't be home tonight—I'll be staying with some boys down in the Mission district." She rolled her eyes. "No way."

"No, silly." Amanda leaned against the wall. "We'll tell her you're staying with me."

A knock sounded on the door, and Mrs. Larson stuck her head inside the room. "Honey, I hate to be the bearer of bad news, but Mrs. Brehony just called and—"

"My pictures aren't on the truck," Pepper

finished for her. She looked at Amanda and added, "Surprise, surprise."

"I'm sure you must feel just sick," Mrs. Larson said. "I wish there were something I could do."

Amanda kicked Pepper in the ankle, and Pepper squeaked, "Actually, Mom, there is something."

"What's that, dear?"

"Would you mind if I spent the weekend with Amanda? I just don't think I can sleep in this room after what's happened."

"I don't blame you," Pepper's mother said. "You go right ahead. Just be sure and call me tomorrow to let me know how you're feeling."

Pepper smiled angelically. "Thanks, Mom."

When Mrs. Larson shut the door, Amanda gave Pepper a thumbs up sign. "Way to go," she whispered. "Now, I'll call Mick and make the arrangements."

Pepper flopped on the torn mattress and moaned, "We'll never get away with this. Not in a million years!"

# CHAPTER FIVE

I t was almost midnight when they reached Fleet Street in Pepper's car. Mick Soul stood in the doorway, the collar of his black leather jacket turned up against the chill. The streetlight cast long shadows across his strong-boned face, and he seemed more handsome than ever.

"Not too many girls call me up and ask if they can spend the night," Mick said, smiling his slow half-smile.

Amanda looked him straight in the eye. "We were desperate."

Mick threw his head back and laughed. It was a deep, rich laugh full of warmth.

A stocky guy with dark, curly hair and a pockmarked face stuck his head out the door and grinned at the girls.

"Hi, Gabe," Amanda called. Gabe Sanchez was Mick's best friend and partner, and just about the nicest person Amanda knew.

Mick and Gabe ran their messenger service out of the back room of the Sanchez family grocery store. During the day the room bustled with activity, as riders were dispatched to businesses all over the city.

"Welcome to Hotel Sanchez," Gabe cracked.

"Don't get any ideas, buddy." Pepper dragged her suitcase up to the door. "This isn't a slumber party. We're just here to hide out—and that's all!"

"Don't worry about them," Mr. Sanchez called, as he came around the side of the building. He was carrying a blanket and a large pillow. "They told me about your problem, and I'm going to be right here in the store keeping an eye on things."

"See?" Mick stepped back and gestured to the room that was usually Fleet Street. "We have everything here. Luxurious accommodations, the best security guards you can find—plus a chaperone."

Amanda stepped through the door and smiled. The battered desk with the telephone had been pushed to one side. Two neatly made cots had been set up against the far wall, and a small table holding a lamp stood between them. A clothesline was strung across the room with a brightly colored bedspread draped over it.

Mick patted the bedspread and said, "This is for your privacy." He pointed to the beat-up old couch on the other side of the room. "Gabe and I will bunk there."

"Both of you?" Amanda raised an eyebrow.

"Naw," Mick replied with a chuckle. "I'll sleep on the couch, and Gabe'll take the floor."

"No way, man," Gabe called from the door. "We said we'd flip for it."

Mick shrugged and pulled out a quarter. He flipped it in the air with his thumb. "Call it."

"Heads!" Gabe shouted.

The coin hit the floor and Mick flashed a smile of victory. "Like I said, I take the couch, and Gabe gets the floor."

"I think I just threw my back out," Pepper wheezed as she heaved her suitcase over the doorsill into the room. She started to drag it across the floor when Gabe grabbed the handle from her.

"Here, let me help you." He tried to lift the large leather case. "What've you got in here—a bowling ball?"

Pepper put her hands on her hips. "Very funny. I packed a few clothes—"

"A week's worth," Amanda corrected.

"And my photo albums."

Amanda rolled her eyes. "She has this idea that the thieves will come back and steal the pictures of her in elementary school."

"Well, they're irreplaceable," Pepper retorted. "I mean, I've got pictures of my first five birthday parties in here."

"What happened to the last twelve?" Mick asked.

Pepper shrugged. "Mother got bored with arranging birthday parties for me, so we went out."

Mick turned to Amanda. "Where's your suitcase?"

"Right here." She patted the leather backpack looped over her shoulder. Amanda had tucked a pair of blue jeans, a shirt, and a sweater into one compartment, and her nightgown and toothbrush into the outside pocket. Many years of traveling with her parents had taught her to pack light.

Gabe half-carried, half-dragged Pepper's suitcase over to one of the cots. "Don't put this thing on the bed," he advised. "It may break it."

Pepper stuck her tongue out at him. "Don't worry. I won't." The girls stood side by side at the foot of their cots, facing the boys.

"Uh, well, it's getting pretty late," Mick finally said. "And you guys must be tired."

Amanda nodded. "Yeah, we've had a long day."

"We can talk about everything tomorrow," Mick said as he and Gabe backed away to the other side of the room. "And in the meantime, if you need anything, just whistle—I'll be over here on the couch."

"And the floor," Gabe added.

"And in the store," Mr. Sanchez reminded them from the outer room.

"Thanks, you guys," Amanda said. "We really appreciate this."

Mick winked at her. "Hey, no problem."

There was another pause. Finally Amanda said, "Well, good night."

"Good night," the boys chorused.

She pulled the flowered bedspread across the clothesline until the boys were gone from view. "It's weird," she whispered to Pepper, "knowing they're just across the room."

Pepper knelt by her suitcase. "I'm glad they are. After what's happened today, I feel a lot safer."

She was answered by a male voice. "Thanks, Pepper."

The girls looked at each other in alarm. Then Amanda peeked her head around the bedspread. "Can you hear us?"

"Of course." Mick had flopped down on his back on the couch. Gabe was piling cushions into a makeshift pallet on the floor. "That's just a curtain, you know. It's not a wall."

"Well, it's not polite to eavesdrop," Amanda said primly.

"So don't talk," Mick shot back. He saluted jauntily, and Amanda flipped the drape shut.

Pepper unlocked her suitcase, and it flew open with such force that she fell backward onto the floor, letting out a loud shriek.

Mick was beside them in a flash. "What's the matter?"

"Her suitcase exploded." Amanda pointed at the books strewn on the floor around Pepper's cot.

Pepper dug through the pile of clothes and photo albums and pulled out a nightshirt that looked like a long football jersey. "Aha, here it is." She clutched it to her and said pointedly, "I need to put it on."

Amanda and Mick ducked under the clothesline, pulling the bedspread across behind them so Pepper could change in private. Amanda lowered her voice. "Mick, maybe we should talk now."

He nodded. "I was just about to suggest the same thing."

Amanda met his eyes. "This whole business of the Coop and Pepper's house getting robbed is really making me jumpy." She shuddered. "I wish I knew who was doing it, and why."

Mick reached out and touched her cheek. "Don't worry," he whispered. "We'll do everything we can to find out."

The touch of his fingertips against her skin sent a feeling like an electric shock all through her body. She was suddenly filled with an overwhelming urge to fold herself into his arms. Amanda leaned her cheek into his hand and closed her eyes.

"Hey!" Pepper's voice cut through the air. "What's going on out there?"

Amanda's eyes popped open, and she stiffened. "Nothing, Pepper. I'm just thirsty. I think I'll get some water."

Mick put his hand on her elbow. "Can I buy you a drink?" He chuckled at the confused look on her face and added, "We're in a grocery store, remember?"

"Oh, that's right." Amanda laughed as Mick offered her his arm and escorted her to the front of the store. Pepper called out after them, "While you're at it, bring me a diet soda!"

"And a root beer," Gabe chimed in.

Mr. Sanchez was checking the lock on the front door when the two entered the store. "What's the matter?" he asked. "Can't sleep?"

Amanda nodded. "Yes, it's hard to keep everything from swirling around in your head."

"I told Mandy I'd buy her a soda," Mick explained, reaching into the refrigerator case. "To calm her down."

Mr. Sanchez smiled. "I'll put it on your account."

"Thanks." Mick patted him on the shoulder affectionately. Mr. Sanchez settled into the recliner that sat behind the cash register and flicked on a little reading lamp attached to the arm. He picked up a dog-eared paperback novel and said, "Think I'll get back to my mystery. I've got to see if the hero and his girl get out of the jam they're in."

"Good night, Mr. Sanchez," Amanda said.

"*Hasta mañana.* See you in the morning."

Taking Amanda by the hand, Mick led her to the front of the store. "Okay," he said, sitting on the window seat. "I got the basic facts over the phone. Now give me the details."

Amanda closed her eyes and methodically recited the events of the day. When she'd finished,

Mick was silent for quite a while. Finally he spoke. "I think we can be sure of two things. One—all of these incidents are related."

"What's two?" Amanda asked, taking a sip of her soda.

"Whoever's doing it means business."

His tone was deadly serious, and Amanda felt a chill run up her spine. "I hope we haven't gotten you involved in something too dangerous."

"I don't know," Mick drawled. "If it takes a crisis to get to see you again, it's worth the danger."

Amanda blushed and said quickly, "You know what I mean."

"Don't worry." Mick touched her arm lightly. "Gabe and I can take care of ourselves. And we'll be watching out for you."

The lights were off in the back room when the two of them returned. Mick felt for a flashlight that he kept on top of the safe and flicked it on. At the same moment Amanda stumbled into a chair. "Oops. I'm afraid I'll wake the others."

Mick shone his light across the room. "Don't worry about Gabe." Mick pointed at the huge lump snoring softly on the couch. "He's already asleep. And on my bed!"

Amanda couldn't help giggling. "Serves you right."

Mick led her to the clothesline that divided the room. "Well, I guess this is *really* good night."

Amanda nodded. Then she did something that

surprised her. She stood on tiptoe and brushed his cheek with a kiss. "See you tomorrow."

Before Mick could respond, Amanda slipped behind the curtain. She got undressed in the dark, felt for her nightgown, and pulled it over her head. Amanda smiled to herself as she listened to Mick humming softly across the room.

When she slipped under the covers and finally lay her head on the pillow, a voice beside her said, "Okay, Hart, where's my soda?"

"Sorry, Pepper," Amanda whispered. "I forgot. I guess I was thinking about something else."

"Yeah." Pepper yawned. "And his initials are M.S."

Amanda shut her eyes and sighed. "Good night, Pepper."

# CHAPTER SIX

## E

|arly the next morning the gang huddled around the desk in the back room at Fleet Street, eating the hot breakfast rolls Mr. Sanchez had thoughtfully brought them.

Mick took a sip of his coffee. "Okay, you think someone's out to get Pepper and her pictures. Have you got anyone in mind as a suspect?"

Amanda set her roll down on the paper plate and wiped her hands on her napkin. "We're pretty certain it's got to be one of the other three finalists in the photo contest."

"Pepper, if you win this contest, what do you get?"

"Five hundred dollars and lots of camera supplies," Pepper replied. "And a medal," she added with a grin.

Gabe whistled under his breath. "Not bad for a contest."

Mick picked up a pad of paper lying next to the telephone. "Give me the finalists' names."

Pepper scratched her head. "I only met them for a second. Let's see. Richard Reely was there with his family—the original Chub Club. They weighed in at about a thousand pounds each. Then there was a jerk named Martin Watts—he acted like a real know-it-all. And the other contestant, I think her name is, uh, Susan Wan."

"What's she like?" Mick asked.

"I don't know. She wasn't there."

Mick raised an eyebrow. "Not at the opening of her own photo show?"

"Sounds suspicious to me," Amanda said, taking a sip of her coffee. "While you were at City Hall she could have been trashing the Coop and robbing your house."

"Any idea where they live," Mick continued, "what schools they go to, stuff like that?"

Pepper shook her head and reached for another cinnamon roll. She paused in midair. "Wait a minute. My mom cut the announcement out of the paper. Maybe there's something in there." She picked up her purse and pulled a tiny piece of newsprint out of her billfold. "Here it is."

Pepper handed the paper to Mick, who read out loud, "Susan Wan, daughter of Hiram and Betty Wan, attends Sunset High, where she is very active in the Glee Club, FHA, and the Youth Symphony."

"That's a vicious criminal if I've ever heard one," Gabe quipped.

Mick shrugged. "You never know. I say we call her." Before anyone could protest, he had picked up the phone book and opened it to the Ws.

"What are you going to say?" Amanda asked as Mick scanned the page and wrote down a number.

"I don't know," he admitted as he punched in the phone number. "I'll see what happens when they answer."

"What if you have the wrong Wan?"

"I'll hang—uh, hello, is this Mrs. Wan?" Mick sat up straight in his seat. "May I speak to your daughter Susan?"

Amanda came up beside Mick and put her ear to the receiver.

"Oh, I'm sorry to hear that," Mick said. "She's been in bed for how long? Well, that must be why I didn't see her at the Picture the City opening." Mick listened for a few minutes longer, then said, "No, I guess I'll just call back later. Thank you, Mrs. Wan. And I hope Susan gets better."

He hung up the phone and faced the others. "Susan Wan is out. She has mono and has been in bed for two weeks."

"Well, that narrows the field," Amanda said. She picked up the clipping and read, "Richard Reely works at Playland at the Wharf—"

"You've got to be kidding," Pepper murmured. "He runs those bumper car rides?"

"Either that or he sells cotton candy," Mick said with a chuckle.

"Maybe he's a bouncer," Gabe threw in. "If he's as big as you say he is."

Pepper made huge sweeping motions with her hands. "Bigger. *Much* bigger."

"And Martin Lionel Watts," Amanda said, raising her voice to carry over theirs, "is an overachiever. He's president of the Science Club, Chess Club, and Russian Club at Leland High, and is the founding officer of the Shutterbug Society."

"Shutterbug?" Pepper stuck her finger down her throat. "I wonder if he picked that name himself."

"Why don't we ask him?" Amanda said, standing up and brushing the crumbs off her lap.

"What, call him?" Mick asked.

"No, I think we should go see Martin. In person."

"Now?" Pepper asked.

Amanda shrugged. "The sooner, the better." She held up the clipping. "The paper says he'll be giving a lecture in Golden Gate Park this morning."

"That's my idea of fun," Mick cracked.

Amanda put her hands on her hips. "Well, if we're going to get to the bottom of this, don't you think we should talk to the suspects?"

"But . . . but I need to work on my pictures," Pepper protested. "I've got to get to a darkroom."

"Why don't you set one up here?" Gabe said. "You can use the storage room. It's got a sink.

And you'll be safe." He crossed his thickly mus-
cled arms. "I guarantee it."

"I'll need some supplies," Pepper said, taking
the last bite of her cinnamon roll. "Developing
chemicals, my enlarger, some photographic
paper—I've got to get to a photo supply store."

Mick shook his head. "You shouldn't go out.
We'll send someone."

Amanda moved to the corner where the cots
were and put on her coat. "Well, I, for one, am
going to the park."

Mick leaped to his feet. "I'm going with you."

"Why don't you take Mustang Sally?" Pepper
tossed him her car keys. "It'll be faster that way."

Amanda took two steps toward the exit and
froze. Someone was at the back door trying to get
in. All eyes turned to the exit, where they
watched the door shake.

Pepper ducked behind her chair while Mick and
Gabe moved silently to each side of the door,
ready to pounce on the intruder.

There was a loud thunk as the person outside
kicked at the door.

"Oh, no!" Pepper moaned.

Suddenly, the door flew open, and the front
end of a ten-speed was thrust into the room. That
was followed by a slender Asian teen dressed in
snug cycle shorts and a warm-up jacket. He
unstrapped the white bike helmet from his head,
and Mick and Gabe relaxed visibly at the sight of
his long, black ponytail.

"Terry!" Mick greeted him. "What are you doing here?"

"I figured since it was Saturday, I'd do some work on my bike." He rolled the ten-speed over to the far corner of the room, where a workbench had been set up. "The gears keep jamming up on me."

"Man, you scared us!" Gabe leaned his back against the wall.

"Scared is putting it mildly," Pepper said, coming out from behind her chair. "My heart is still pounding."

Amanda put her head on the desk. "I thought we were finished for certain."

"Terry, I want you to meet some friends," Mick said. Terry propped his bike against the wall and faced the group with his hands on his hips. A thin, jagged scar running down the side of his face glowed bright red from the wind.

"Terry Han, meet Amanda Hart—"

Amanda nodded. "Hi, Terry."

"And Pepper Larson."

"Pleased to meet you," Pepper said brightly.

Terry stared at them, his face unsmiling. There was something unsettling about the intensity of his gaze. Amanda felt as if her measure had been taken, and she was found lacking. Finally he grunted something that sounded like, "Hi."

"Terry, before you get started," Mick said, putting his arm around the wiry boy, "I've got a little job for you."

After Mick explained about the photographic supplies, Amanda looped her arm through his and said, "And *I've* got a little job for *you*."

"And what job is that?" Mick asked.

"We have a date, remember?" Mick's eyes brightened for a moment, and then Amanda explained, "With Martin Lionel Watts."

Less than an hour later, Mick and Amanda stood by the boat house on Stow Lake at Golden Gate Park. Around his neck Mick wore a pair of beat-up binoculars that Gabe's father had lent him. Amanda wore one of Pepper's camera bags over her shoulder. She hoped that made it look as if she knew something about photography.

The park was filled with joggers, tourists, and families out for weekend picnics. But the area around the boat house was deserted. Amanda pointed to the park service sign. "It says the Shutterbug Society meets at ten. Where is everybody?"

"Everybody got smart and left," Mick cracked. "If we had any brains, we'd do the same."

"Now hold on." Amanda grabbed the sleeve of his jacket. "It was your idea to interview the contestants."

"On the phone," Mick corrected. "You're the one who thought we should attend this boring event."

"How do you know it's boring?

"The *Shutterbug Society*? Give me a break."

Mick did an exaggerated yawn. "Just saying the name makes me tired."

A shrill whistle pierced the air, and Amanda covered her ears. "What was that?"

Mick flipped his sunglasses down on his nose. "That, my dear, was Martin Lionel Watts."

He pointed to the front of the boat house, where a skinny boy in thick glasses stood with his hands on his hips. He wore a vest with pockets for film and filters, and a huge camera hung around his neck. A bulging camera bag sat on the park bench next to him.

"Hello, fellow shutterbugs," the boy announced in a high, squeaky voice. "And welcome to this week's meeting. I'm Martin Watts."

"Bingo," Mick murmured under his breath.

Martin read from a note card that he clutched in both hands. "It is so good to see all of you today."

"All of us?" Mick looked over both shoulders. "What is he, blind?"

"No." Amanda giggled and nudged Mick in the ribs. "Just nervous."

Martin cleared his throat noisily. "Um, some of you may be aware that I have been selected as one of the finalists in the Picture the City photo competition."

Amanda applauded politely, and Martin beamed. "Thank you, thank you. My entry— which I have titled, Hide in Plain Sight—is currently on display in the rotunda of City Hall until after the final judging, when it will move to the lobby of the de Young Museum here in Golden Gate Park."

Mick cupped his hands around his mouth and shouted, "That's *if* you win."

"Well, of course." Martin adjusted his glasses and squinted at Mick. "But I am by far the most experienced photographer of the finalists and, well . . ." He chuckled self-consciously. "I know the judges."

"What!" Amanda protested. "That's not fair."

"It's perfectly fair," Martin replied. "Mine is simply the best entry, and the judges, who are all professionals, will recognize that."

"He seems awfully sure of himself," Amanda murmured to Mick.

"Yeah, that jerk's too cocky to steal someone else's work. We can probably scratch him off our suspect list."

Martin shuffled through his cards and continued his speech. "I chose to document how the common killdeer avoids detection from its predators by building its nest right out in the open. Today I'll discuss with all of you the techniques I used to get my photographs."

"I can't wait," Amanda groaned.

Mick shook his head. "Can you believe this guy? He hasn't even noticed that there are only two of us here."

Amanda suddenly found herself stifling a

yawn. "I wish this were over with. Richard Reely has got to be more entertaining than Martin."

Mick took her by the hand. "Why wait to the end? Let's just leave now."

Amanda's eyes widened. "But that would be rude. What will he think?"

"I promise you," Mick whispered, "Martin will never see us leave. And if he does, we'll just tell him we're at the wrong meeting." He held up his binoculars and cracked, "We're looking for the Happy Trails nature walk."

A group of joggers thundered down the sidewalk toward the boat house, and as they passed, Mick and Amanda joined them. Behind them they could hear Martin droning, "By using a combination of high-speed film and a depth of field determined by the use of lower-than-normal f-stop settings . . ."

As Martin's voice faded in the distance, Amanda glanced up at Mick and chuckled. "I think we just witnessed the last meeting of the Shutterbug Society."

# CHAPTER SEVEN

T̲hat's him. He's the one we're after."

Mick gestured with his thumb to the heavyset boy running the baseball toss at the amusement arcade.

The boy walked up and down behind the long counter, making change and handing out balls and prizes. He was wearing a blue canvas apron that had "Playland at the Wharf" printed on it in bright orange letters.

"How can you tell?" Amanda asked, as they wove their way through the noisy maze of brightly flashing pinball machines and video games. In the center of the arcade a tiny, riderless carousel circled around and around, accompanied by organ music.

"His name tag says Richard, and Pepper said he was huge." He grinned and added, "She wasn't kidding. This guy could pass for the Pillsbury doughboy."

Amanda peered at Richard from behind a giant scale that promised to tell both weight and fortune. "He doesn't look like a thief. I think he looks really friendly."

"Looks can be deceiving."

The two of them watched carefully as Richard cheered for a young boy who managed to knock all the dolls down with his first toss. He handed him a large fluorescent pink poodle.

"You'd have to pay me to take that thing home," Mick cracked.

"It is pretty ghastly," Amanda agreed with a giggle. "But the little stuffed gorillas are kind of cute." She pointed to a shelf of them perched behind another booth, called Sweethearts' Toss. Each little ape was wearing a different type of hat.

"You want a gorilla?" Mick flipped up the collar of his jacket with a confident flick of his wrist. "I'll get you a gorilla."

"Mick!" Amanda grabbed his arm as he started to walk over to the counter. "Remember what we're here for."

"I won't forget," Mick said. "But there's no harm in having a little fun while we're on the job."

He sashayed up to the curly-haired blond behind the counter and declared, "My girl wants a gorilla. How do I win one?"

His brash words caught Amanda by surprise. Did he really mean she was *his* girl? Or was that just part of the act? Amanda felt her cheeks turn bright red. She hoped he didn't notice.

"It's real easy," the counter girl explained, holding up a wooden hoop painted to look like a diamond engagement ring. "You toss one of these onto the ring finger of any of those hands back there—and you get a gorilla."

Mick stared at the larger-then-life-size plaster hands placed about ten feet from the counter. "Piece of cake." Mick grinned at Amanda and paid a dollar for three rings.

Twenty minutes, and twenty dollars, later Mick searched his pockets for another dollar bill.

"Mick, forget it," Amanda said. "It's not worth the trouble."

He shook his head stubbornly. "Once more. I'll get it this time, I promise."

The blond girl behind the counter held out one of the stuffed gorillas. "Take it, it's yours," she urged. "I mean, you paid for it three times over."

Reluctantly Mick took the doll. "I don't get it. I always win at these games."

He stared in mute frustration at the little gorilla with the baseball cap on its head. The red-and-yellow lights of the arcade cast a soft glow on his face, and Amanda had a sudden glimpse of what he must have been like as a little boy. Mick had never looked more endearing. "I wish I had a camera," she said.

"You asked for it, you got it," a merry voice answered behind her. There was a bright flash of light and the whirring of an instant camera. Amanda turned to see the boy named Richard

Reely pulling the exposed film off its cartridge. "Usually I charge a dollar for a Polaroid," he said, as he handed her the developing print. "But this one's on the house."

Amanda watched as the picture of Mick holding the gorilla slowly came into view. The photographer had caught his expression perfectly.

"Thank you," she said with a pleased smile. "I'll treasure it forever."

"Say, Mandy, I'll make you a deal." Mick held out the tiny stuffed animal. "The gorilla for the picture."

Amanda stepped back, holding the photo out of reach. "What are you going to do with the picture?"

"Burn it," he said emphatically. "I can't let something like that get out. It'll ruin my reputation."

Amanda raised her hand and swore solemnly, "I promise I won't show it to a single soul. Except maybe Pepper." She paused. "And Gabe." She hesitated again. "And my cousin Josh, when he gets back."

"That does it!" Mick marched back up to the counter. "I'm giving back the gorilla."

"No!" Amanda protested, grabbing for it. Mick lifted the stuffed animal out of her reach, and the flash went off again. "Yeow!" Mick blinked and rubbed his eyes. In that split second Amanda snatched the gorilla out of his hands.

"Thanks for the diversion." She giggled as she

ducked behind Richard Reely's imposing bulk.
"Now I've got them both."

Mick glared at them, his arms folded across his
chest. "Come on, big guy," he pleaded with
Richard, "don't give her another picture. She'll
blackmail me with it for sure."

"I won't," Richard replied as he slipped the
photo into his shirt pocket. "This one's for my
collection. I keep a record of all the faces I like
that come through Playland." He turned and took
a quick close-up of Amanda. "It's kind of a hobby
of mine."

Abruptly Mick and Amanda snapped to attention as they remembered their real mission.
Amanda put on her best investigative reporter
voice and said, "It's more than a hobby with you,
isn't it?"

Richard cocked his head in confusion.

"Aren't you Richard Reely," Mick jumped in,
"one of the finalists in the Picture the City
contest?"

Richard Reely's eyes widened in surprise.
"Why, yes, I am. How did you know?"

"We read it in the newspaper," Amanda replied
just as Mick said, "We caught the exhibit at City
Hall."

They stared at each other, then Amanda
turned to Richard to explain carefully, "*After* we
read about it in the newspaper, we went to see
your show at City Hall."

"That's it!" Richard snapped his fingers. "I

thought you looked familiar. I never forget a face. Like I said, I collect them."

Mick jumped on his words. "How about other people's photos? Do you collect them, too?"

Richard was taken aback by the vehemence of Mick's question. "Wha-what do you mean?" he stammered.

"I imagine you take a great deal of interest in other people's work," Amanda said sweetly. "As a professional, that is."

Richard chuckled pleasantly. "Aw, I'm not a professional at all. This is just a hobby. I never show my pictures to anyone."

"What do you mean, never?" Mick said quickly. "You entered that contest, didn't you?"

"Well, actually, I didn't," Richard confessed. "My sister entered me. At first I was kind of mad that she'd do something like that without my permission." He smiled and added, "But when I made it to the finals, I was pretty excited."

"I would be, too," Mick said. "Five hundred dollars is a lot of money."

"I guess." Richard leaned against a pinball machine and slipped a new film cartridge into his camera. "I'm just flattered someone thought my pictures were any good."

Amanda raised an eyebrow. "You're not interested in the money?"

"Oh, sure. So's my sister. I promised I'd give her half if I win."

"Whoops!" Amanda deliberately dropped the

gorilla doll on the ground. As she bent over to pick it up, she was momentarily hidden from Richard's sight by the counter between them. She gestured for Mick to join her. When he knelt down she whispered, "I don't think it's him."

Mick nodded. "Me, either. I'm betting on his sister."

The two stood back up at the same time, broad smiles on their faces.

"So," Amanda said brightly, "what does your sister plan to do with her share?"

"I don't know," Richard replied. "Why don't you ask her?" He pointed at the curly-headed blond who ran the ring toss and had given Mick the little gorilla. "Hey, Peggy," he called, "these folks want to know what you're going to do with the prize money if I win."

Mick and Amanda looked from the gargantuan Richard to the petite blond, and back again.

"How could those two ever be related?" Amanda whispered under her breath.

"Strange genetic mutations," Mick replied with a straight face. Amanda had to cover her mouth to keep from giggling.

Peggy folded her arms on the counter and said, "I think the first thing I'll do is have my hair straightened. Then I'll buy some new tapes, maybe get a new sweater. How about you?"

Richard's list was as mundane as his sister's.

Amanda whispered, "People don't plan elaborate robberies just to have money to get their hair done."

"You're right," Mick muttered out of the corner of his mouth. "Let's motor."

While the two siblings compared shopping lists, Mick and Mandy slowly backed out of the arcade. When they reached the door, Amanda called out, "Thanks for the picture, Richard!"

"And the souvenir." Mick held up the gorilla. "It's been real."

Outside on the waterfront, Amanda sighed. "I'm sure neither one of them would ever steal anything."

"Yeah." Mick ran one hand through his hair. "That pretty much wraps up the theory that a jealous contestant is out to get Pepper."

"It's looks like we're back to square one." Amanda shivered in the crisp breeze and pulled her suede jacket close around her.

Mick nodded. "We don't know who stole Pepper's pictures, or why."

Amanda cocked her head and looked at him. "So now what do we do?"

"I say we head back to Fleet Street and regroup."

Amanda pointed to a little street vendor's cart with a striped awning parked near the corner. "Why don't we get something hot to drink first?"

"Sounds great but—" Mick turned his pockets inside out. "You're going to have to treat. That gorilla busted me."

"Piece of cake," Amanda said, using Mick's words. She flipped up the leather flap on her purse and pulled out two dollars. "Two cappuccinos, please."

The man poured two tiny cups of espresso, then poured them into larger plastic cups, which he filled to the brim with frothy steamed milk. As a final touch he sprinkled a dash of cinnamon on top.

They carried their drinks over to the water's edge, and Mick raised his cup in salute. "I'd like to propose a toast. Here's to you and—" Mick paused dramatically—"the gorilla."

"To the gorilla," Amanda repeated, tapping her cup against his. As the two of them sipped the warm, tasty coffee, their eyes met in a long, steady gaze. Mick took her arm in his, and without speaking they strolled down the promenade toward the car. At the newsstand on the corner, Mick stopped and said softly, "This has been fun."

Amanda nodded. She liked the feel of his arm holding hers and didn't want to break the moment. Mick added with a twinkle in his eye, "Expensive . . . but fun."

Amanda giggled. Then something behind Mick's shoulder caught her eye.

"Mick, look." She reluctantly took her hand from his arm and picked up one of the papers on the newsstand. She read the headline out loud.

"Witness in Chinatown Murder Disappears. Conviction of Gang Leader Willie Chow Unlikely."

"Too bad." Mick took the paper from her and scanned the article. "I think they really thought they were going to nail the Chairman this time." He frowned. "No wonder they say he's untouchable."

"You know about all this?"

"Who doesn't? Willie 'the Chairman' Chow's the most vicious gang leader in the city—controls most of the dope coming in. Word is he's connected to one of the Triads in Hong Kong."

Amanda shook her head. "Triads?"

"Chinese organized crime syndicates. From what I've heard, they make the Mafia look like a bunch of Cub Scouts."

Amanda took a final sip of her cappuccino and swallowed hard. "How weird! I was there at City Hall yesterday when the police brought him into court." They dropped their empty cups into a trash can and headed for the car. "I had no idea it was so important!"

"Yeah, everyone in the city is watching this one. Convicting the Chairman could break the wall of silence that seems to protect these crooks."

When they reached the yellow Mustang, Amanda asked, "How come you know so much about it?"

"Terry Han." Mick unlocked her door and held it open. "He used to run with a street gang in

Chinatown, but got out when they started working for Willie."

"Terry was a drug dealer?" Amanda asked uneasily. She thought of Terry's scarred, unsmiling face and shuddered.

Mick shook his head. "Like I said, he got out. Terry's a good guy. He's had his problems, but he's clean. I trust him."

A staccato burst of sharp explosions ripped through the air, and Amanda shrieked. Without thinking she threw herself into Mick's arms. "That sounded like gunshots!"

Mick folded his arms around her protectively. "Relax." His lips brushed her forehead as he said softly, "It's just fireworks."

Another round of explosions rocked the air, and he pointed toward some boys down by the water's edge. "It's Chinese New Year, remember? It's been like this for two weeks."

"I guess I'm a little jumpy," Amanda confessed as she slid into the passenger seat. "None of what's happened makes any sense."

Mick hopped in the driver's seat and started the engine. They pulled out of the parking lot and headed for Fleet Street. Just after they crossed the intersection a white van appeared in the lane ahead of them. Amanda realized with horror that it was headed the wrong way.

"Look out!" she cried. "It's in our lane."

Mick hit the horn, but the van kept coming.

"He's trying to kill us!" Amanda screamed and covered her face.

Out of desperation Mick drove the car off the street onto the sidewalk. The right wheel jolted up over the curb with a crunch, narrowly missing a mailbox, and the car came to a stop. The van swerved back into its lane and roared off down the street.

Mick leaned his head against the steering wheel. Tiny beads of sweat lined his forehead. Amanda struggled to calm her pounding heart. Finally she whispered, "That was no accident."

She could barely hear his murmured reply. "I know."

# CHAPTER EIGHT

I t took only a few minutes to drive back to Fleet Street, but after their near head-on with the van, it felt like an hour. They parked the Mustang in the corner lot and hurried down the alley. Amanda followed Mick to the door and froze.

"What's the matter?" Mick asked.

"It's too quiet," Amanda replied, still not stepping into the room. "Isn't anybody here?"

"I don't know." Mick cupped his hands around his mouth and shouted, "Hey! Anybody home?"

Pepper's muffled voice came from the storeroom. "I'm in here!"

Amanda raced to the door and pulled on the knob. It refused to budge. A thousand horrible images raced through her mind—the robbers had come to Fleet Street while they were gone, beat up Pepper, thrown her in the storeroom, and left her for dead. "Mickey, it's locked!"

"Well, of course it's locked," Pepper's voice came clearly from the other side of the door. "I don't want you to come in."

"Pepper?" Amanda hissed. "What's wrong?"

"Nothing. It's just not a good idea to have anyone come in when I'm developing my pictures." The lock clicked, the door opened, and Pepper squinted out into the light. "But it's okay now. They're done."

Pepper had on her usual baggy pleated jeans and bright tie-dyed T-shirt. Over that she wore a big white apron from the grocery store. She untied the apron strings and looped it over her head. "What took you guys so long? Gabe and I were starting to get worried."

"Gabe," Mick said. "Where is he?"

"Up front with his dad."

Amanda and Mick exchanged relieved looks, and Amanda said, "Well, I'm just glad you're all safe and sound."

Pepper studied her friend's face. "What happened out there? You don't look so good."

Amanda sat in the overstuffed chair. "I feel great, considering we were nearly killed."

"By Martin Watts?" Pepper gasped.

"Naw." Mick waved his hand. "That guy is the ultimate nerd. He couldn't steal your pictures, because he's barely aware they exist."

Amanda nodded. "And Richard Reely is just too nice a guy."

Pepper stared at Amanda. "You said you were nearly killed. Were you kidding?"

Mick shook his head. "Someone in a white van

tried to run us off the road. We narrowly missed hitting a mailbox."

Pepper's eyes widened, and Amanda added, "Don't worry. Your car's all right."

"Forget my car. Are you two okay?"

"A little shaky," Amanda said, "but all right."

Mick handed Pepper the car keys from his pocket. "We parked the Mustang in the corner lot. And just as a precaution, I think it should stay there."

"Wow." Pepper sat down on a wooden chair by the door. "This is too weird for words."

Amanda patted her friend on the arm. "You're telling me. First someone steals your pictures, then they ransack the Coop and your room, and now they're trying to hurt you."

"Me!" Pepper squeaked.

"Well, yes," Mick said. "They probably thought it was you driving the Mustang."

"That does it." Pepper stood up and faced Mick and Amanda. "I've come to a decision. I'm dropping out of the contest."

"Pepper, you can't!" Amanda cried. "That's just what they want."

"Hey!" Pepper held her hands up in protest. "If someone wants me out of the contest that badly, I'll quit. It's not worth it."

"First of all, you've worked too hard to just drop out." Amanda crossed her arms firmly in front of her. "And second of all, if you drop out, we'll never know who's doing all this. Or why."

Pepper slumped back in her chair. "There's another reason I need to drop out."

"What other reason?" Amanda peered into her friend's face.

Pepper gestured to her darkroom, where nine wet prints could be seen hanging from clothespins on a line stretched across the room. "Without the tenth picture, my entry just isn't any good."

"Do you remember where you took the picture?" Mick asked. When Pepper nodded, he said, "Well, why don't you just reshoot it?"

"It wouldn't be the same. I'll show you what I mean." Pepper gestured for them to join her in the darkroom. "You see, I took each shot at a certain time of day."

Mick and Amanda peered at the pictures. Each was of a different location, with words and drawings scrawled on the crumbling side of a brick building, or an overpass, or the edge of a playground.

"If you'll look closely, you'll see how the light advances across each wall, as though the sun was the painter."

Mick nodded appreciatively at Pepper. "I'm impressed."

"They're terrific," Amanda added. "It looks like you used time-lapse photography."

"It wasn't time-lapse, but time did elapse," Pepper joked. "Seriously, it took hours of waiting to get that effect. You can see how hard it would be to reshoot it."

"These are great by themselves," Mick said. "Why not enter just these?"

Pepper shook her head so hard, her glasses fell down to the tip of her nose. "That's not the way I pictured my entry. It needs the last shot to make it complete. A sunrise-to-sunset effect. Otherwise, it's garbage."

Mick shrugged. "You're the artist."

Amanda moved back to the end of the line and examined each picture. Standing in the tiny room, surrounded by the smell of darkroom chemicals, Amanda was suddenly hit with a wave of nostalgia. "This really reminds me of my parents."

"The pictures?" Pepper asked.

"No," Amanda replied. "The whole thing. The plastic tubs filled with chemicals. The little red light overhead. I remember when Mom and Dad would go over each one of their photos, arguing which would be the perfect shot for Mom's articles."

As photojournalists, Del and Dinah Hart were famous the world over. They'd twice won the coveted Pulitzer Prize, for their reporting of the Vietnam War and the conflict in Northern Ireland.

Mick, who was standing behind her, murmured, "You must really miss them."

Amanda nodded. "Especially on days when I see my life pass before me." She wiped her eyes self-consciously. "It's silly."

Mick put a comforting hand on Amanda's shoulder. She felt foolish for becoming so emotional and hurriedly changed the subject. "Uh, Pepper, why'd you choose these particular shots?" Amanda pointed to one of the pictures. "I mean, there's graffiti all over the city."

Pepper cocked her head. "I guess I liked the overall design of them. Each one seemed to have a unique message—"

"Jason loves Jenny," Mick read out loud. "You call that a message?"

Amanda grinned at him. "I'm sure it was a very important message to Jenny."

"No, I mean it. They each have a special drawing in them." Pepper unclipped two pictures from the line. "See, this freeway overpass is covered in a rainbow. And the water tower has those huge eyes painted on it."

Amanda examined a third photo. "What about all these strange squiggles along the bottom?"

Pepper leaned in closer. "Oh, those. I think they're the artist's signature."

"Artist?" Amanda repeated.

"Sure. Graffiti artists each have a mark or design that's their personal signature. They leave it everywhere."

"That's true," Gabe said, joining them and glancing at the photos. "But the ones you're pointing at look a lot like the way street gangs mark their turf."

"Street gangs!" Amanda and Pepper exclaimed at the same time.

"Sure," Mick said. "You ever see that old movie, *West Side Story*?"

Amanda nodded. "With the Sharks and the Jets."

"Each of those gangs had its own territory," Mick continued. "It's the same thing here. Only these gangs are a lot tougher than those wimps in the movie."

"This guy doesn't look so tough." Pepper pointed to a corner of one print. A boy of about fourteen was looking furtively over his shoulder at the camera, a can of spray paint in his hand. "He was terrified that I'd caught him spraying the wall."

"I don't blame him," Gabe said. "It was bad luck that you caught him on film."

Mick nodded. "Yeah, what if some cop sees your exhibit and then recognizes this kid on the street? The cop could bring him in and use the picture for evidence."

"On what charge?"

"Vandalism." Mick ticked off the charges on his fingers. "Willful destruction of property, making a public nuisance."

"What policeman's going to see her pictures?" Amanda scoffed.

"What cop's not?" Mick shot back. "I mean, they were hanging right there in City Hall."

"Well, if what you say is right," Pepper said

swallowing hard, "this guy would have a motive to get back at me."

Amanda sat up straight in her chair. "Wait a minute."

"Uh-oh." Pepper examined her friend's face closely. "Stand back. The light bulb just went on in Amanda Hart's head."

Amanda leaped to her feet and paced around the tiny room. "Maybe we've been looking in the wrong place. Maybe what Pepper said is true."

They stared at her blankly. "Come *on*, Mandy," Mick urged, "fill us in."

She made a sweeping gesture to the photos hanging on the clothesline. "Maybe the answer's been in front of us the whole time and we just didn't see it." She looked at the others. "Maybe our thief doesn't want Pepper out of the contest. But he wants her *pictures* out of sight."

"You mean there might be something in one of my shots he doesn't want anyone to see?" Pepper asked.

Amanda nodded, and the four friends clustered around the photos to look more closely.

"But which picture?" Gabe murmured.

"Why don't you each take two photos," Amanda said, moving to her back pack, "and write down anything you think might be unusual or odd." She tore sheets of paper from her lavender notepad and handed them around. "Then we'll switch pictures and see what we come up with."

Each one of them took a couple of photographs and a piece of paper and retired to a corner of the back room. Amanda sat at the desk while Pepper flopped into the overstuffed armchair with the torn seat.

The back door swung open, and Terry Han came into the room. "Hey, Mick, you going to need me for anything else today?"

Mick shook his head without looking up from the photos in front of him. "No, thanks, man. Hey, have a good weekend."

"We'll see you Monday," Gabe echoed as he squinted at his pictures. "Bright and early."

"Okay." Terry went over to where his ten-speed was hung on a hook from the ceiling. He took it down and set it back onto its wheels. Amanda noticed him watching them all intently out of the corner of his eyes. He fiddled with the gears for a moment, then put the wrench away abruptly.

"Okay. I give up," Terry declared, turning to face the others with his hands on his hips. "Is someone going to tell me what's going on around here, or do I have to guess?"

Amanda glanced over at Mick anxiously. She didn't know if Terry could be trusted. But Mick jumped in and told Terry about the theft of Pepper's photo essay, the robbery at her home, and the white van running them off the road. "At first we thought it had to be one of the finalists in the contest, but we checked them all out. No way could they have done it. They're not the type."

Gabe moved back to the card table, where he'd left his photos. "Mandy thinks there might be something in one of these pictures that someone doesn't want people to see."

"Like this guy with the paint can." Mick held up his photo. "Or maybe there's a hidden message—something that might be incriminating—in the graffiti." He held it out to Terry. "What do you think?"

Terry took the picture and sat on the arm of the couch. "It looks like your standard stuff. Chicano, Anglo . . . street rap, you know? They even threw in a few Chinese characters."

"Really?" Amanda put her picture down and joined Terry and Mick. "Do you know what they mean?"

Terry pointed to one corner. "These characters say, *sing fat.*"

Amanda studied the brush strokes. "Does that have a special meaning?"

Terry nodded. "'Expanding prosperity.' Around New Year every wall in Chinatown is plastered with phrases like this."

"Take a look at this one." Amanda handed him the photo of the bridge overpass that she had been examining.

Terry pursed his lips and shook his head. "I don't read Chinese very well." He pointed to a different series of scrawled designs. "But I know these. They're names of street gangs."

"What did I tell you?" Gabe called from the card table.

"Those are for the Young Dragons. That's the Band of Steel." Terry waved his hand over some other symbols. "These look familiar, but I couldn't tell you what they mean." He handed the photo back to Amanda. "Probably good luck, or something dumb like that."

Amanda narrowed her eyes at the picture. "But what if they mean something else? Something important. We can't afford to overlook anything."

Pepper nodded. "We need to find someone to translate."

"That's easy," Terry said with a shrug. "My grandmother's from Hong Kong. She could do it."

"All right!" Mick gave him a low five. "I knew we could count on you."

"How soon can we see her?" Amanda asked.

Terry scratched his head. "Tomorrow would probably be fine. She usually has tea in the early afternoon. You could visit her then."

"Tomorrow?" Pepper muttered. "Does that mean we have to spend another night here?" She turned to Gabe and Mick. "No offense, but that cot is not exactly comfortable."

"Try sleeping on the couch," Gabe said. "Each lump feels like a giant fist."

Mick raised one hand. "Want to trade? The floor doesn't have any lumps."

"Maybe we should just go back to my house, Pepper," Amanda said, thinking of her cozy room and warm bed.

Mick shook his head. "No way. After what happened today, you're going to have to stay here. At least till after we talk to Terry's grandmother."

"What about your mom?" Amanda asked Pepper.

"I talked to her this morning. She said it's better that I don't come home right away. The house is full of guys installing the new alarm system."

"You told her you were staying here?" Amanda asked wide-eyed.

"Are you nuts?" Pepper choked. "She still thinks you and I are having a grand old time watching movies and eating pizza at your house."

"I wish we were," Amanda said sighing wistfully.

Mick bowed to Amanda. "Your wish is my command." He moved to the desk and picked up the phone. "I'll call for a pizza. And, Gabe, see if your dad's TV still works."

"That almost sounds like fun," Pepper said as she collected her photos.

"Yeah," Amanda said, trying to be optimistic, "we should look at this like sort of an urban camp-out."

"Maybe we could make one of those great Girl Scout concoctions," Pepper said eagerly. "We'd need chocolate, graham crackers, and marshmallows."

Amanda giggled. "Now all we need is a campfire."

Mick pulled out a butane lighter. "With a little imagination, this might work."

Terry, who by this time had wheeled his bike to the door, shook his head. "You guys are too weird for words. I'm out of here."

# CHAPTER NINE

O n Sunday afternoon Mick and Gabe led the girls to Chinatown on their borrowed bikes.

"I cannot *believe* I let you talk me into this," Pepper said as she struggled to pedal up the steep incline of California Street. "First, my whole body is one big soreness from sleeping on that cot for two nights in a row. Then . . ." She paused, gasping for breath. "Then Mick gets the bright idea that we should disguise ourselves as bike messengers, and wear these stupid bike helmets and goggles. And you *agreed* with him."

Amanda, who was on a rickety ten-speed ahead of Pepper, panted, "It's a perfect cover. I just never *dreamed* that riding a bike in San Francisco was so difficult." She raised her head and shouted to Mick and Gabe, who were pumping easily to the crest in front of them, "Don't go so fast, you guys."

At the top of the hill the boys pulled over to the curb. Amanda and Pepper crawled up beside them. Pepper hit the brakes too hard and jerked off her seat. Then her bicycle helmet fell forward over her eyes. This sent Gabe and Mick into fits of laughter.

Pepper pushed the helmet back off her forehead. "I give up!"

"You can't give up now, *chica*!" Gabe patted her on the shoulder. "We're almost there."

"I've got an idea!" Pepper said, forcing a cheery smile. "Let's call a cab with a bike rack."

Amanda, who had finally managed to catch her breath, called, "I'm with Pepper!"

"Relax, you two," Mick replied with a grin. "It's all downhill from here. But we've got to step on it. Terry's supposed to meet us by the market, so follow me and stay close."

He turned and coasted off down the hill. Amanda followed, grateful that gravity was now doing the work. The bike began to pick up speed as they rolled past Grace Cathedral and the landmark hotels of Nob Hill. It was all Amanda could do to keep her balance. Mick and Gabe led them in a wide swing to the left, taking them through a tight maze of apartment buildings. Finally the group coasted to the edge of the Chinese market, and Mick raised one hand, gesturing for them to stop.

"I'm glad that's over with," Amanda said, her eyes still stinging from the wind. "I was afraid I wouldn't be able to stop."

Although it was Sunday, the market was clogged with shoppers, jostling their way between the stalls of exotic vegetables and meats.

The air was thick with a rich, pungent smell that was almost overpowering.

"We'll walk from here," Mick said. "No riding through all of that."

They pushed their bikes through the crowd. Everyone around them seemed to be talking at once and at the top of their lungs. Rows of golden glazed roast ducks hung on hooks in the open air next to racks of dried fish.

"I think I'm going to gag!" Pepper moaned suddenly.

"What's the matter?" Amanda cried out.

Pepper pointed at a fish seller who stood by a large saltwater tank filled with squirming eels and octopuses. As they watched, the seller reached a pronged stick into the tank and yanked out a huge gray octopus, which he dropped into the open sack of an eager customer.

"I've just become a vegetarian," Pepper declared.

Amanda laughed, and they pressed on toward the boys, who had slipped a few yards ahead of them.

Terry Han was waiting near the entrance to the market. Amanda was the first to spot him leaning against a wall talking to several tough-looking boys. Amanda realized that if she weren't with Mick, she would have been afraid even to walk by that group.

"There he is," she murmured to Mick.

"Yo, Terry!" Mick shouted over the crowd.

Terry raised his head and nodded, then murmured something to his companions, who disappeared down the alley.

"My grandmother's ready to meet you," Terry said without so much as a smile or hello. "She's already made tea."

Before Amanda could answer, Terry had already headed away at a brisk walk. "Follow me," he called over his shoulder.

Mick and Gabe followed Terry closely, but Amanda and Pepper had to jog to keep up with them. It was particularly difficult since they still had their bikes. They passed from one narrow lane to another, each one darker and more mysterious than the last. Amanda tried to keep track of each twist and turn, but soon realized that she was hopelessly lost.

"It's hard to believe this place exists right in the heart of a modern American city," Amanda marveled. "We could be in a foreign country."

"You are," Terry muttered in a low voice. "And don't forget it."

Amanda was taken aback by the harshness in his voice. She stopped walking and asked, "What do you mean?"

Mick saw the hurt in her eyes and explained in a gentler tone, "Chinatown has always been kept separate from the rest of San Francisco, with its own laws, government, police—everything."

They continued down another alley with elaborately carved balconies in dragon and lion motifs. Terry swung open an iron gate and gestured for them to follow him into the narrow courtyard. "Put your bikes in there." He pointed to a small utility room. "Then we'll go upstairs."

Terry pressed the doorbell, and then a buzzer sounded. He pushed open the door, and the air was suddenly filled with the fragrant aroma of oranges and mint.

"That smells delicious," Amanda said, closing her eyes and taking a deep breath.

"My grandmother likes incense." Terry led them up a flight of plushly carpeted stairs. "Especially around New Year's—the house always smells this way."

They entered a small sitting room with wooden tables of inlaid teak and mahogany. A richly designed china tea set sat on the center table, with six little cups ringing the teapot. Thickly cushioned settees covered with embroidered silk brocade were scattered around the room.

"Make yourself at home," Terry announced. Then he disappeared through a beaded curtain into the interior of the house.

Suddenly Amanda felt a little nervous. She smoothed back her hair, trying to make her appearance look a little neater after the wind-blown bicycle ride. "Have you got the pictures, Pepper?"

Pepper pulled a portfolio out of the rucksack she had been carrying on her back. "Right here. We're all set."

The beaded curtain rustled, and Terry came back in. A thin, birdlike woman clung to his arm, her slippered feet padding softly on the carpet. With great gentleness Terry helped her over to one of the settees, where the old woman settled into the cushions with obvious relief.

Terry sat down beside her and then said to the others, "This is my grandmother, Naomi Han."

They introduced themselves, and then Amanda said, "I'm not sure how to start this, ma'am. You see, we've—"

"Please don't call me ma'am," the old woman interrupted, her voice surprisingly vigorous and youthful. "You'd think I was an old bag with one foot in the grave."

Amanda looked at Mick in surprise, then all of them burst out laughing. Amanda realized it was the first time she had ever seen Terry smile.

"You—you speak English?" Pepper exclaimed.

"And Chinese, French, and a little Spanish. Languages are pretty simple once you get the hang of them." She clapped her hands together gleefully. "Now, let's have some tea."

Mrs. Han poured them each a cup of steaming tea, and as they sipped it, she described what it was like coming over from Hong Kong fifty years before. "Of course, when I left Hong Kong, it was just a little backwater town. Nothing like it is today."

The old woman set down her cup. "I know why you're here. Terry tells me you've got a mystery to solve." Her black eyes glittered merrily. "I *love* mysteries! So, please, let's get down to business."

Pepper pulled her pictures out of the portfolio as Amanda explained what they were looking for. Mrs. Han examined each one carefully. "There's quite a bit of repetition here. Characters for luck, some numbers, dates, a lot of animals."

"Animals?" Amanda asked.

"Yes, tigers, dragons, and so forth."

"Gangs," Terry murmured.

"Right. We went over that before," Pepper said, glancing at Gabe.

"Do you see anything like a specific message in any one of these photos?" Amanda persisted.

The old woman shook her head. "It's just a lot of gibberish." She turned to Pepper and asked, "Why did you take these pictures, anyway?"

"Well, I thought the drawings were kind of artistic."

The old lady arched a skeptical eyebrow. "This is what I would call urban blight, not art."

"That depends on how you look at it," Pepper said. "See, I was riding on the cable car last fall, and as I passed a bunch of these walls, the patterns in them caught my eye. They were like abstract art, you know? So then I rode back over the route and took a shot of each one again. And I liked them so much, I decided to branch out and see what other designs these street artists were doing."

"Wait a minute, Pep," Amanda exclaimed. "The ones you shot from the cable car—did you use any of them in your display?"

"Sure. Four of them."

Amanda picked up the sheaf of prints. "Which ones?"

Pepper pulled out three prints and set them on the tray. "These three." She grimaced and added, "The fourth one is the one negative the thief stole from the darkroom—"

"Pepper, listen to me," Amanda interrupted. "Put them in the order you saw them from the cable car."

Pepper stared at her, then shrugged, and did as she was told.

"What are you getting at, Amanda?" Mick asked quietly.

"What if it's not just one of Pepper's pictures that holds the message, but a series of them all put together?"

Mick's eyes widened. "I get it. Someone might see a piece of the message, but it wouldn't mean anything without the other pieces."

"And unless you knew where to find the others—" Gabe jumped in.

"You'd never crack the code," Amanda finished.

Pepper handed the pictures to Mrs. Han. "This is the way I saw them. What do you see?"

Mrs. Han looked them over carefully. Finally she nodded and said, "Here, here, and here. See that?" She pointed to a corner in each of the pictures. "Different Chinese characters—but all by the same hand."

Amanda set her teacup on the table. "What do they say?"

"Well, here we have the character *ta*—that means big. And the sign for snake. Big Snake. Then there's a date."

"What is it?" Mick stood behind Amanda with his hand on her shoulder.

Mrs. Han shook her head. "It's in the Chinese calendar. Let me think . . . In the Western calendar, that would be October twenty-ninth of last year."

"And the next picture?" Mick urged.

"Some numbers—threes and sixes—lucky numbers for Chinese. And a time—the first hour after midnight."

"One A.M.," Amanda murmured. "What about the third shot?"

Mrs. Han stood up and shuffled to the corner, where a tall brass lamp with a red-and-gold fringed lampshade stood. She pulled the chain and held the photo up to the light. "This is the character for a mongoose. And here is a new number." She squinted at the photo. "Four-two-six."

Terry spoke sharply. "What did you say?"

Mrs. Han looked at him in surprise. "Four-two-six, Terry."

"Is that something important?" Amanda asked quickly.

"I thought . . ." Terry hesitated, then shook his head. "It's nothing."

Mrs. Han shuffled back to the table, where she picked up the last photo. "This one is easy," she said, smiling at the group. "It's a place—the Street of Painted Balconies."

"That's Waverly Place," Terry exclaimed, "right here."

"Is that a special address?" Amanda asked.

"The seat of traditional power in Chinatown," Mrs. Han explained. "All of the Tongs have their headquarters there."

Pepper reached for her third powdered cookie and asked, "What's a Tong?"

"It's hard to describe," Terry said. "They started out as secret societies to protect local Chinese from persecution and help them survive here. They ruled Chinatown business life completely for a long time."

"Now they're like big corporations," Mick added.

"And still very powerful," Mrs. Han remarked with a frown.

"Here's what we have so far." Amanda read from the notes she had written on her pad. "Something about a big snake and a mongoose, some lucky numbers, a date, a time, and a location."

"Sounds like a message to meet someone," Mick noted.

"Like for a drop," Terry said.

"A drop?" Pepper asked, dabbing her mouth with a napkin.

"A drug exchange." Mick pursed his lips in thought. "If this is what it looks like, a dealer could communicate with his street runners right out in the open, and no one would suspect a thing." He shrugged. "Who reads graffiti, anyway?"

"Just like Martin's entry—hide in plain sight," Amanda mused, chin in hands. "I'll bet the clue that ties it all together was in that last photo of yours, Pepper."

Mrs. Han touched Terry lightly on the arm, and he nodded. "My grandmother is getting tired," Terry Han announced. "I think it's time to leave."

"This was invigorating. I hope I was of some help," Mrs. Han said as they bade her farewell. "Please let me know if there's anything else I can do."

"You've been invaluable." Amanda shook her hand gratefully. "Now it's up to us to put it all together."

As they were retrieving their bikes, Amanda noticed Terry pull Mick to one side and murmur something in his ear. Mick's eyes widened with surprise.

"Thanks for letting us talk to your grandmother," Pepper called to Terry. "She's great. And so are her cookies."

"Sure." He looked up and down the alley warily. "Listen, you guys, take care."

"Why?" Amanda asked. "What's going on that we don't know about?"

Terry stared at her, and for a moment Amanda thought she could see a glimmer of fear in his eyes."

"We'd better motor," Mick said abruptly. "It's time to get off the streets." Amanda shot him a questioning look, and he said, "I'll explain when we get back to Fleet Street."

The group bicycled back in silence, replaying Mrs. Han's words in their heads. When they finally reached Fleet Street and carried their bikes up the back steps, Pepper gasped. "I can't believe we made it." She headed straight for the couch and flopped facedown on the cushions.

Amanda removed her bike helmet and sat down in the chair. Every part of her body was sore. "Okay. *Now* can you tell us what the mystery is?"

Mick made sure the door was locked behind him before he turned to face the group. "Terry didn't want to say anything in front of his grandmother," he explained. "But there was something in those messages she translated that worries him."

Amanda stopped massaging her aching calves and nodded. "That number—four-two-six. Right?"

"Yeah," Mick acknowledged. "You see, that kind of numbering is used by the Triads to identify their members."

"Wait a minute." Pepper rolled onto her side. "I just got used to Tongs. Now we're into Triads? What are they?"

"Chinese Mafia," Mick said. "Based in Hong Kong."

"And they wrote the book on dirty drug dealing," Gabe said, handing each one of them a soda from the front of his dad's store. He shook his head. *"Muy malo.* Very bad."

Amanda took a long, cool drink of her cola. "So what's that got to do with Pepper's pictures?"

"I don't know," Mick admitted. "Maybe nothing. Maybe everything. Terry's going to check that number out on the street. He'll call us when he knows what's going down."

"So what do *we* do?" Amanda asked. "Just sit here?"

"Right. We sit tight and stay out of sight. He'll call as soon as he knows anything."

The rest of the afternoon crawled by at a snail's pace. Shortly after dark Gabe went and got them a dinner of homemade tamales from his mother. By ten o'clock it was clear Terry was not going to call.

When Amanda slipped under her blanket on the cot, she tried hard to quell the doubt she felt inside. Although Mick seemed to trust Terry,

Amanda sensed a bottled-up tension in the young Asian-American that was unnerving.

"Mandy?" Pepper's voice whispered softly in the dark.

"Yes?"

"I hate this waiting around."

"Me too."

"If I had a camera, we could go get another shot of that missing wall tomorrow morning. I know exactly where it is. We could sneak back here and develop it, and the whole thing would be solved."

Amanda smiled. "I think that's a great idea. Your car's still at the corner lot, right?"

"Right. And there's Mr. Mooney's old camera in the Coop at Sutter."

"First chance we get tomorrow, you grab the car, and we'll leave. But don't breathe a word of this to Mick or Gabe. They'd never go for it."

Pepper chuckled. "You took the words right out of my mouth."

# CHAPTER TEN

T|he next day Amanda paced anxiously on the curb in front of the grocery store. It was Monday afternoon, and Gabe and Mick were in the back, hard at work dispatching their Fleet Street messengers. The girls had been waiting patiently all day for just the right moment to slip away unnoticed.

"Hurry, Pepper," Amanda whispered.

A throaty rumble announced the arrival of the ancient yellow Mustang. Pepper pulled up to the curb, and Amanda leaped into the front seat. "Let's go!"

Pepper popped the clutch, and the force of the car pulling away from the curb threw Amanda back against the seat.

"I said go, not blast off!"

Pepper grinned and swiftly maneuvered them out of sight. "Mick's going to be pretty torqued when he finds out we've gone."

"Well, he shouldn't be," Amanda replied. "It's our life. We're free to do what we want, aren't we?"

"If you say so."

Twenty minutes later, Pepper turned the car into the alley behind Sutter Academy. The burbling sound of Pepper's muffler echoed among the quiet buildings. Amanda winced at the noise they were making. "I knew there was a reason you should have fixed that muffler."

Pepper stuck out her tongue in reply, but promptly cut the engine, and they coasted silently up to the Coop. They both got out and tiptoed to the side of the building. Amanda peered around the corner and looked up at Sutter's main campus, which sprawled a hundred yards away. No one was stirring in the courtyard, called the Hub.

"Everyone seems to be in class," she whispered. "Remember, we're supposed to be sick, so don't let anyone see you."

The two girls scurried around the side of the building and up to the door. Amanda fumbled in her purse for the key.

"No one's fixed the window," Pepper hissed, pointing to the shattered glass on the ground.

Amanda unlocked the door, and they slipped into the darkened room.

"Don't turn on a light," Amanda warned. "Someone might see it and come investigate."

Pepper tripped over a box of paper that lay on the floor. "I don't think anyone's been in here since it got trashed on Friday."

"Don't worry about the Coop. We'll deal with it

later," Amanda said, as she waited for her eyes to adjust to the dim light. "Just get the camera, and let's go."

"That's not as easy as it sounds. Mr. Mooney has a strange way of filing things."

"Don't you know where it is?" Amanda asked. "I would think the staff photographer for the *Sutter Spectator* would know where to find the school camera."

"I never use it," Pepper said, as she rummaged through one of the cupboards. "It's old and a piece of junk."

Amanda put her hands on her hips. "Then what are we doing here, Pepper? If someone saw us, we could get expelled."

"Yeah," a voice agreed from the doorway. "Miss Wilson will forgive almost anything but cutting classes."

Pepper shrieked and clutched Amanda. Amanda automatically felt behind her on the desk for the scissors. Then the lights came on, and Peter Yang stepped into the room. As usual, he was impeccably dressed, in a tailored blue blazer, light gray wool slacks, and charcoal cashmere sweater. Gold cuff links gleamed from the wrists of his button-down shirt.

"Relax," he said. "I just wanted to get a copy of last week's issue."

"Peter! You scared the living daylights out of me!" Pepper said, hurriedly smoothing her hair. Amanda watched the blush go to her friend's cheeks at the sight of the handsome senior and wondered if she was that obvious whenever she had a crush on a guy.

"Wow! What happened here?" Peter asked, surveying the wreckage.

"Some vandals thought they'd do some redecorating," Amanda said, trying to make a joke of it. She moved to the closet where the back issues of the *Spectator* were stored, pulled out a copy of the latest issue, and handed it to Peter.

"Vandals!" Pepper exclaimed. "We're talking about vicious thieves out to get me and my pictures."

Peter cocked his head. "So that's why you guys are skipping classes."

Amanda spun to face him. "Who said we were skipping?"

"The usual gossips on the Hub at lunchtime." Peter smiled easily. "They figured since both of you were gone, something must be up."

"Well, we had a few things to do, regarding the next issue of the paper, and—"

"Come on, Mandy," Pepper interrupted. "We can tell Peter."

"Tell me what?" His eyes glittered with interest.

Pepper made sure no one was outside the door, then said in a low voice, "Remember when I saw you at City Hall, and my entry was missing?"

"Yes. They thought it had been been packed by

accident on a truck to New York with some other stuff."

"Well, it was moved all right—right out of City Hall, and maybe out of the country!"

Amanda rolled her eyes at her friend's exaggeration.

"You see," Pepper continued breathlessly, "there must be something in one of my pictures that's incriminating—a message or a code. Mick thinks it may be a signal for a drug drop."

Peter looked at her curiously. "Who's Mick? Does he go to Sutter?"

"No. He's just a friend," Amanda said quickly, "who's helping us figure this out. In the meantime, we're keeping out of sight until we know what's going on."

"I see." Peter perched on the edge of the table. "Sounds pretty exciting. Anything I can do to help?"

"Actually, there is," Amanda said. "Would you talk to Miss Wilson for us?"

Peter shrugged. "Sure. What do you want me to say?"

"Tell her we're investigating a great story for the paper, and we're wrapping it up today."

"Do you think she'll believe that?" Pepper asked.

Amanda smiled. "She will if Peter tells her. You know, senior class president . . . straight-A student . . . voted most likely to succeed. How could she *not* believe him?"

Peter bowed to Amanda. "Thanks for the vote of confidence. Meanwhile, what are you two planning to do?"

"Get out to the North Beach playground. If I can find the beat-up box that Mr. Mooney calls a camera, we're going to try to get another shot of one of the graffiti walls. It might hold the key to the whole puzzle."

"I thought you said that camera didn't work," Amanda said.

"Oh, it works all right," Pepper said as she opened some boxes by Mr. Mooney's desk. "It just doesn't work well."

Peter stood up. "Where would he keep it?"

"He has an unusual system for filing things," Amanda explained, "that no one can ever figure out. Like, if it's pencils—most people would look in the box labeled *P*, right?"

Peter nodded.

"Well, he keeps his pencils under *L*. For lead."

"As opposed to *I* for ink pens," Peter said.

"Exactly." Pepper beamed at Peter.

"So that means it wouldn't be under *C* for camera," Amanda said.

"Did you try *F* for film?" Peter suggested.

"That might work." Amanda went to the file cabinet. "But it might be too obvious." She stopped and chewed thoughtfully on a fingernail. "Pepper, what is it Mr. Mooney is always calling the camera?"

"The third eye."

Amanda snapped her fingers. "Check under *T*."

Pepper pulled a chair over to the far storage closet, where shelves held shoeboxes with different labels. She stood on the chair and reached for the box marked *T*.

"Ta da!" She opened the lid and held up a battered camera. "We can go." Pepper nearly lost her balance, but Peter stepped in quickly to steady her.

"Careful, Pepper, you could hurt yourself." He put one hand on her waist and offered her his other hand.

Pepper took it gracefully and batted her eyelashes behind her wire-rims. "Thanks, Peter."

He helped her down, saying, "Look, if what you say is true, you two should be extra careful out there."

"We will," Amanda said, tugging at Pepper to hurry her up. "And thanks again, Peter, for talking to Miss Wilson for us."

"No problem."

Amanda walked to the door and looked out cautiously. A student was crossing the parking lot to his car. She waited for him to back out and drive away, then gestured for Pepper to follow her.

"Bye, Peter," Pepper sang out as they headed for the alley and the waiting car.

"Bye, Peter," Amanda repeated once they were out of earshot, imitating her friend's high-pitched voice.

Pepper punched her on the shoulder. "Did I really sound like that?"

"Worse. But it's okay." Amanda hopped into the front seat of the car. "I think Peter feels the same way about you."

"Do you really think so?" Pepper giggled as she started the engine and pulled out of the driveway.

Amanda smiled. "Really." She turned to Pepper. "I wonder what he was doing out of class."

"Probably had important school business to attend to," Pepper replied. "I mean, he's not only class president, but a member of Student Council and the student liaison committee to the faculty." She turned to Amanda and added, "Say, did you know Peter also has a black belt in kung fu?"

Amanda chuckled. "Let's just say Peter's perfect, and leave it at that." She picked up the old camera and examined it. "Wow, this is pretty messed up. Do you think it'll work?"

"Sure." Pepper glanced at it briefly. "At least it's got film in it. I don't know how much, but all I need is one shot."

In a few minutes they reached the corner of Mason and Columbus. "That's it." Pepper pointed across the intersection at the tennis and basketball courts of the North Beach playground. She pulled over to the curb and double-parked by a fire hydrant.

"We can't park here," Amanda protested. "We'll get towed."

Pepper was already out of the car and crossing the street. "So find us a parking spot, will you?"

"Pepper! You know I don't really drive!"

But Pepper was already out of hearing range. Amanda sighed and climbed into the driver's seat. She gritted her teeth as she shifted to first gear and the car jerked into traffic. Luckily a delivery van pulled out of a loading zone right in front of her. Amanda guided the Mustang into the slot and parked. She turned on the blinkers and hurried after her friend.

She found Pepper slumped miserably on a fire hydrant with her face in her hands.

"What's the matter?"

"It's gone." Pepper pointed to the side of the brick building. Part of the wall had been turned into a clever mural showing people playing sports using golf clubs for bats and footballs for baseballs. The rest of the wall was covered in graffiti.

"It's been painted over." Pepper pointed to a rectangular patch of black spray paint obscuring the bottom right-hand edge of the wall. "I think what we wanted was under that."

Amanda tried to swallow her disappointment. "Well, maybe you should take a picture of the wall anyway, just in case there's something else we've overlooked."

She offered her friend a hand and pulled her to her feet. Then Pepper backed as far away from the wall as she could and aimed the camera. The shutter clicked, and Pepper automatically advanced the film. "Hey, it looks like we've got one more picture," she said, examining the counter.

"Here." Amanda took the camera from her friend. "I'll take a close-up of this lettering. It's kind of unusual."

Amanda moved to the side of the red recreation building and got down on one knee to get a good angle. Suddenly, running footsteps sounded behind her. She turned just in time to see a young boy in a hooded sweatshirt grab Pepper around the neck. He was dragging her toward the street.

"Mandy, help!" Pepper choked, flailing with her hands to break the thug's grip. She kicked and squirmed, but couldn't get her footing.

Amanda ran to help her just as the thug bumped into the fire hydrant and stumbled backward. He sprawled onto the grass, still clutching Pepper. Amanda swung the camera by its strap as hard as she could into the guy's hooded face, and he howled in pain. At the same time Pepper managed to pry his fingers loose from her neck. Amanda jerked Pepper to her feet and shouted, "Run!"

The two of them tore off down the street, not knowing where to turn. Amanda could hear footsteps running after them, and panic crept up into her throat. They turned the corner, and the green-and-white awning of a little grocery store appeared before them. Amanda grabbed Pepper's hand, and they ducked inside.

"Is he still—?"

Amanda clapped her hand over Pepper's mouth. Footsteps pounded down the pavement outside, then stopped. There was a brief pause, then they faded away down the street.

Amanda released her hand, and Pepper gasped for air.

"He must have run the other way," Amanda whispered. "We're okay for now."

"Oh, God, Amanda, he was trying to kidnap me!" Pepper was shaking violently with fear. "We . . . we could've been killed!"

The girls wrapped their arms around each other and held tight. It was only then that Amanda realized their assailant could have had a knife, or a gun. She had attacked him without thinking about the consequences—and she was so glad she had.

"Pepper," Amanda whispered. "I think it's time to call the police."

# CHAPTER ELEVEN

S|ergeant Rubano twirled the edge of his moustache as he listened to Amanda and Pepper describe the attack. The policeman beside him furiously scribbled notes. They were standing in a tight knot on the playground when Mick arrived on his ten-speed. He braked to a halt in a spray of gravel just a few yards away.

Amanda looked over at Pepper, who whispered, "I called him. I thought he should know."

Leaving Pepper with the detective, Amanda walked over and joined Mick.

"What's the idea of sneaking off without telling me?" Mick snapped, his blue eyes flashing steel.

Amanda stiffened at his angry tone. "My, aren't we in a good mood."

Mick ignored her sarcasm. "Well?"

"We had to go to the school to get a camera," she replied evenly. "And I didn't think you'd go for that idea."

"You're damn right I wouldn't," he said between clenched teeth. "What is this, a game to you?"

"I don't know what you mean."

"One minute you and Pepper are afraid for your lives and need a place to hide out. The next, you're off cruising your school like you don't have a care in the world."

"We're running out of time, Mick. I thought it was worth the risk."

"Have you lost your mind? Or do you want to get killed?" Mick ran his hands through his hair. "I told you I'd try to protect you. But you apparently felt you didn't need my help." He gestured in disgust at the police cars and the small crowd that had gathered. "If you'd listened to me, none of this would have happened."

"If I'd listened to you, we'd still be sitting at Fleet Street, waiting for Terry Han to call us."

"Well, at least you'd be safe."

Amanda turned on her heel and marched back to join Pepper and Sergeant Rubano.

"Did you get a look at this guy's face?" the sergeant was asking.

Pepper shook her head. "He grabbed me from behind."

"He had on a gray sweatshirt jacket, with the hood pulled tight around his face," Amanda said. "I would say he wasn't much taller than Pepper. Pretty scrawny."

"Anything else?" Sergeant Rubano asked. "Think really hard. The slightest detail might give us something to follow." He shook his head wearily. "Right now, we've got nothing."

Amanda carefully replayed the sequence of events in her mind. The boy dragging Pepper down the sidewalk. His tripping over the fire hydrant. His cry as the camera hit his head. Pepper tearing at his hands to pry them off . . .

"I do remember something!" Amanda shouted. "He was wearing a ring." She shut her eyes tight, trying to picture it. "It was gold and had the head of an animal carved on it. Like a cat."

"A cat." Sergeant Rubano toyed with his moustache thoughtfully. "Could it have been a tiger?"

Amanda remembered the cat's mouth being open in a snarl. "Yes. I think it was."

Sergeant Rubano and the policeman exchanged knowing looks.

"What does that mean?" Amanda asked.

Sergeant Rubano pointed behind her at Mick, and his voice turned suddenly harsh. "Ask your friend here. He hangs out with those punks."

Amanda looked at Mick in dismay. She'd had no idea that he knew the detective. Mick tossed his head defiantly and stared back at Sergeant Rubano.

"Ask him!" the detective repeated, pointing at Mick with his finger. "Ask him about Terry Han. Terry Han, who's got a list of juvenile offenses as long as my arm."

"Rubano, you lay off Terry!" Mick shouted. "He quit the Tigers over a year ago. He's been clean ever since—and you know it!"

Sergeant Rubano flipped up the collar of his coat. "Why should I believe you?"

"Because I'm telling the truth. Or doesn't that matter to you?"

"Read my lips," the detective snapped. "Terry Han's a bum. Got it? You hang out with him, you're a bum, too."

Amanda watched their argument with a growing sense of horror. In the past, whenever the police appeared, Mick disappeared. There had to be a reason for it. And why was Mick protecting Terry Han?

Panic welled up inside her, and Amanda felt an uncontrollable urge to run away. It didn't matter where, just so long as she could escape from the doubt gnawing at her insides. She turned and dashed across the playground.

Mick and the sergeant were still shouting at each other when Mick spotted Amanda slipping away. He raced after her and caught her by the sleeve of her sweater.

"Where do you think you're going?" he demanded.

"Away from you," she cried, "away from this mess—everything!"

"Hold on." Mick put both hands on her shoulders and made her look at him. "You tried that this morning, and Pepper nearly got kidnapped."

"What did you have to do with that?"

"What are you talking about?" Mick's eyes were cloudy with confusion. Then he glanced over his shoulder at the two policemen. "Oh, that business with Rubano. Is that it?"

"Yes." Amanda's voice sounded shaky and timid in her ears. "What was he saying about Terry Han?"

"Look, I told you Terry used to run with a street gang—the Tigers. They're mean, no question about it—one of the toughest in the city. But, believe me, he's not with them anymore."

Amanda searched his face. "But how does the sergeant know you?"

Mick closed his eyes and sighed. "That's a long story." When he looked at her again his gaze was open and honest. "Let's just say I haven't exactly led a sheltered life. Where I come from, crime is a recreational activity."

Amanda knew so little about Mick. Now was her chance to find out who he really was.

"Where do you come from?" she whispered. "Why won't you talk to me about it?"

Before Mick could reply, a newspaper was suddenly thrust between them. "Look, you guys," Pepper shouted. "The police officer had a Sunday paper in his squad car. My picture's in the pink section for the photo contest."

The pink section was the entertainment part of the Sunday paper. It listed the upcoming week's events, theatre reviews and human interest stories in the arts.

"Oh, great!" Mick threw up his hands. "Now everybody can identify you."

"Let me see that." Amanda took the paper from her friend and examined the photo. The four finalists stood smiling behind their entries. "This is almost identical to the one we're running in the *Spectator*."

"Only the one in the *Spectator* is just of me, holding up my pictures," Pepper said. "I look pretty goony, too."

"I thought you looked kind of cute," Amanda protested. "And we got a pretty good shot of your entry."

Mick raised an eyebrow. "The whole entry?"

"Of course," Amanda said. "We took it last Monday."

"All ten photos? Including the one of the missing negative?"

The girls' eyes widened as they realized what he was saying.

"Yes!" Amanda barely breathed the word. She was afraid that a bystander might overhear and guess what they were thinking.

Mick must have been thinking the same thing, because he furtively checked over both shoulders before asking, "And where would this certain shot be?"

"At the printer's—on Howard Street."

A broad smile spread across Mick's face. "What are we waiting for?"

"Let's go get Mustang Sally," Pepper declared. "Where's the car?"

"Just around the corner," Amanda replied.

When they reached the car Pepper gasped in dismay. "What kind of parking job is that?"

The rear of the car was about three feet from the curb, while the right front wheel was resting on the sidewalk. Amanda held up her palms in a helpless gesture. "Well . . ."

Pepper opened the trunk, and Mick put his bike inside. Then the three of them hopped into the car.

"Wait a minute. What about Sergeant Rubano?" Amanda piped up from the backseat. She pointed back at the policemen, who were taking a statement from the owner of the grocery. "Shouldn't we tell him about it?"

Mick checked his watch. "It's after three o'clock now. It'll take at least twenty-five minutes to get to the printer's. What time do they close?"

"Four," Pepper replied.

Mick shrugged. "Okay. You can go talk to Rubano, but he'll mess around, ask more questions, and waste a lot of time. By the time you make it clear to him that you've got to run—the shop will be closed."

"Yeah," Pepper agreed. "And we'll have to spend another night at Fleet Street. I don't think Mom will go for that. As it is, she thinks I've moved in with you, Mandy."

Mick cleared his throat impatiently. "It is now five minutes after three. Do we cruise, or what?"

Amanda made up her mind. "We cruise."

Pepper started to pull out, then stopped.

"What now?" Mick asked in exasperation.

"Well," Pepper said timidly, "Sergeant Rubano did order me to go straight home and not go near a camera or a photo till they straighten this thing out."

"I don't believe this," Mick muttered. *"Drive!"*

His order was so commanding that Pepper stepped on the gas, and they peeled out with a squeal of tires. The noise startled Rubano, and he looked up in alarm just as they drove by.

Mick rolled down the window and shouted, "Yo, Sarge! Something came up, we gotta run!" He tossed off a crisp salute. "Later!"

Mick rolled up the window just as Rubano bellowed his reply. Amanda couldn't hear what he said, but she could tell by his expression that he was less than pleased.

"Step on it, Pepper," she urged. "If we can get there before the shop closes, we'll have that final message."

Pepper bit her lip in nervous concentration. "The picture of my whole exhibit is only an eight-by-ten, but maybe I can blow it up enough to read the message."

"It'll have to do," Mick declared. "Because right now it's all we've got."

# CHAPTER TWELVE ·

I t's closed!" Amanda beat her fists in frustration against the door of the Pickwick Printers.

"It can't be!" Pepper cried. "The sign in the window says they don't close until four. It's only three-thirty."

"They must have closed a long time ago." Amanda peered intently through the glass. "There's not a soul in there."

Pepper kicked at the door. "Maybe we should start thinking about switching printers if they're going to be so unreliable."

"Why don't you call the guy who runs the place?" Mick suggested. "Tell him it's an emergency."

"I would if I could remember his name." Amanda squeezed her eyes shut, trying to concentrate. "You see, his name isn't Pickwick, it's something like Kleinhoff, or Klineman."

"Does that mean we have to wait until tomorrow?" Pepper asked. "I don't think I could take another night on that awful cot."

"You think that's uncomfortable?" Mick chuckled. "You should try the floor."

"I thought you won that toss," Pepper said.

"I did, but Gabe always manages to get there before me." He shrugged. "You try moving a two-hundred-pound sleeping moose."

Amanda shook her head. "I can't remember." Suddenly her hand shot out, and she grabbed Mick's arm.

"What is it?"

Amanda lowered her voice. "The white van—the one that ran us off the road on Saturday—it's here!"

"Oh, no!" Pepper leaped behind Amanda. "Hide me, quick."

Mick bent down to retie his shoe and squinted casually out at the street. "You sure it's the same van?"

"I'd bet my life on it." Amanda barely moved her lips as she spoke. "Oh, Mick, they've parked down at the corner. What should we do?"

"First of all, stay calm. Act casual."

"How can we act casual when I'm going to pass out?" Pepper demanded.

Mick stood up and draped one arm around each girl's shoulder. "Let's just act like we're out window-shopping, having a good time. Now, *laugh*." He threw back his head and laughed loudly.

"What's so funny?" Pepper asked stiffly.

"If you laugh," Mick whispered, "they'll think you don't see them."

Pepper tried to laugh, but a mirthless cackle emerged from her throat. The sound made her giggle hysterically.

"He said to laugh, Pepper," Amanda said, an aritificial smile pasted on her face, "not have a nervous breakdown."

Pepper took several deep breaths, trying to regain control. Finally she huffed, "How could they know we'd be here? We only just thought of it ourselves."

"They must have followed us from the playground," Amanda whispered.

"Let's keep moving," Mick urged them. "Just walk slowly." He led them down the sidewalk past a pastry shop, a tiny boutique, and a grocery. Suddenly he stopped.

"What's wrong?" Amanda asked.

"It might help if you two didn't walk like robots. Loosen up." He leaned in closer to Amanda. "Mandy, put your arm around my waist."

Amanda slipped her hand around his lean, hard waist, and despite the desperate trouble they were in, her skin tingled just touching him.

"Are they still behind us?" Pepper asked.

Amanda leaned her head on Mick's shoulder and peered furtively behind them. "Yes. They're following us slowly down the street."

"These guys mean business." Mick's voice had a

new edge of urgency. "Now, we'll walk for another block, but when I say go—turn right and
run."

"Where should we run to?" Pepper whispered.
"We can't go to my house. They know where I
live."

"Or the school," Amanda said. "They've already been there."

Mick nodded. "We can't take the risk of leading
them to Pepper's pictures at Fleet Street,
either."

"So what do we do?" Pepper asked.

"Let me think." Mick bit his lip in concentration
for a moment. "I've got it. Chinatown!"

"Are you out of your mind?" Amanda protested. "That's like walking right into the lion's
den."

"Exactly." Mick grinned with satisfaction.
"What safer place to be when the lions are out
hunting?"

Amanda stared at him as if he were out of his
mind.

"Look, if those guys in that van really are from
a Chinese gang, the last place they'd expect us to
be is on their own turf."

"And the big New Year's parade happens
tonight." Pepper was warming to the idea. "The
streets should be swarming with people celebrat-
ing."

"You got it." Mick grinned. "It's like that Watts
guy said in the park—hide in plain sight."

"First we have to lose them," Amanda reminded them. "We're nearing the alley."

"Wait a minute." Pepper clutched Mick's arm. "What do we do when we start running?"

"Halfway down this alley is a smaller one on the left that connects with the next alley. It's a tight squeeze that should slow them down a little. At the corner there's a cab stand. Grab the first cab you can find."

"But what if—?"

Mick cut her off. "No time for that. Go!"

Abruptly he shoved the girls ahead of him into the alley, and Amanda and Pepper pounded down the asphalt pavement for all they were worth. Tires screeched from the street as the white van set after them in hot pursuit.

"Heads up." Mick sprinted in front of the girls and ducked to the left into a narrower alley just wide enough to admit a garbage truck parked beside a loading dock.

"We're in luck!" Mick cried. "They'll never get by that."

"Neither will we," Amanda shouted in dismay. There was less than six inches of clearance on either side. Two men were hooking a large green dumpster onto the back of the truck. One of them hit a lever, and the hydraulic lift began to raise the dumpster up onto the truck.

"Follow me," Mick shouted. He ran past the startled men and leaped onto the side of the dumpster. "Come on!" Mick urged the girls.

Amanda spun to see the white van maneuver its way around the corner and speed toward them. The girls exchanged terrified looks and without hesitation jumped up beside Mick, clinging to the green metal for dear life.

"Hey, are you out of your minds? You can't do that!" one of the workers shouted, hitting the lever just before the dumpster reached the top. It lurched to a halt, and Mick hopped down onto the top of the garbage truck. The girls followed suit, and all three of them scrambled down the front of the truck to the pavement on the other side.

"Thanks for the lift," Mick shouted over his shoulder. Amanda could hear the sound of doors slamming and angry voices shouting as they raced down the dark alley toward the light of the street.

They burst out onto the pavement and almost collided with a bright yellow cab. Amanda threw open the door and shouted, "Take us to Chinatown. And hurry!"

# CHAPTER THIRTEEN

**A**s the cab pulled up in front of the Chinatown Gate at Grant and Bush, the sound of hundreds of firecrackers shattered the air. Through the gate the shop-lined street was ablaze with neon light and choked with revelers. Some were carrying tall poles with colorful banners of crimson, yellow, and orange that streamed out over the heads of the people below.

"There must be twenty thousand people here," Amanda shouted above the din.

"At least," Mick replied with a grin. "Talk about getting lost in a crowd!"

"Now that we're here," Pepper asked, "what do we do?"

"We need to find Terry—fast," Mick replied. He gestured to a red phone booth on the corner. It was elaborately decorated with oriental designs that arched in sinuous curves along the panels. "I'll call Fleet Street and see if he's there." He dug in the pocket of his jeans for a quarter. "I want Gabe to come join us, too. We're going to need some more brawn."

"Mick!" Pepper clutched his arm frantically. "Don't leave us out here alone."

"Look, we can't all fit inside this booth," he said reasonably. He glanced around and noticed a little café across the street. "Why don't you two sit over there, where I can keep an eye on you. Don't worry. You'll never be out of my sight."

Amanda and Pepper pushed their way through the crowd across the street into the charming Chinese café, where they grabbed an empty table. They ordered two teas and a plate of cookies. Across the street Amanda could see Mick talking into the receiver inside the phone booth.

The waitress returned with their order, and before she could set it on the table Pepper scooped one of the cookies off the plate. "I just realized I'm starved," she said, taking several quick bites. "We haven't eaten a thing today."

"Careful," Amanda warned, "you're inhaling that so fast, you might choke."

"Eating calms my nerves," Pepper retorted as she bit into the second cookie. A passerby bumped into the back of her chair, and Pepper squealed with fright.

"You call that calm?" Amanda asked, taking a sip of Chinese tea. She didn't mention to Pepper that the tension was having quite the opposite effect on her. The thought of eating anything right now was almost nauseating. Her eyes darted from table to table. Everyone looked suspicious and sinister. Amanda knew that any one of these people could be part of a drug gang pursuing them.

Suddenly Pepper gripped her arm. "Look."

"Where?" Amanda looked around in alarm. "Did the gang find us?"

"No, it's a friend," Pepper reassured her. "Peter Yang just came in here!" Her eyes widened with an odd mixture of pleasure and panic. "What should I do? Say hello?"

"Why not?"

Pepper rolled her eyes. "I don't want him to think I have a crush on him."

"We're running for our lives, and you're worried about a silly crush?"

Pepper looked mortified. "Then I won't say hello."

Amanda spoke softly between her teeth. "You'll have to—he's spotted us, and he's coming over."

Peter Yang was now sportily dressed in pleated blue slacks and a creamy linen jacket. He wove his way through the tables, and a pleased grin spread over his face. "What a pleasant surprise!"

Pepper's face turned a bright crimson. "Hi, Peter."

"Mind if I join you?" He gestured to the vacant chair between them.

"Please do," Amanda replied. She stifled a

smile as she watched Peter shift his chair closer to Pepper when he sat down.

"How did it go today?" he asked.

"Oh, Peter, it was terrible!" Pepper blurted out. "I was nearly kidnapped, that horrible old camera was stolen, and now we're hiding out."

"Pepper exaggerates," Amanda said quickly. "We actually came here because we're trying to find a boy named Terry Han."

"Terry?" Peter raised an eyebrow. "Then you've come to the right place."

"You know Terry Han?" Amanda looked up in surprise.

"Sure." Peter smiled warmly. "We're old buddies. We grew up on the same street. We used to hang out together."

It was hard for Amanda to imagine smooth, suave Peter Yang, the ultimate preppie, being involved with Terry Han. "You two seem . . . so different."

Peter's face grew somber. "We are now. Terry dropped out of school and kind of went his own way. But we still stay in touch."

"Do you think you could help us find him?" Pepper asked.

He nodded. "On one condition."

"What?" Pepper leaned forward anxiously.

A broad smile creased his face. "That you agree to go with me to a movie this Friday."

"What! Me?" Pepper clapped her hands together in delight, knocking over her tea cup. The brown liquid spilled across the table, nearly hitting Peter's linen jacket. Luckily, he leaped up and out of the way in time.

"Can I take that as a yes?" Peter joked as Pepper frantically grabbed wads of napkins out of the metal dispenser.

"I can be such a clumsy jerk," she mumbled, her face red with embarrassment as she dabbed at the spill.

Peter signaled to a waitress to bring a sponge. "Don't worry about it."

"Are you sure you still want to take me to the movies?"

"As long as you don't order anything to drink," he said with a twinkle in his eyes, "I think we'll be safe."

The waitress quickly cleared away the spill. Amanda couldn't help thinking that a date with Peter Yang would be just what Pepper needed as soon as this ordeal was over. But she knew they weren't out of the woods yet. "Can you really tell us where Terry is?"

"I'll not only tell you," Peter replied, "I'll take you there myself."

"Let's go!" Pepper leaped up from her seat.

Amanda nodded and rose to her feet. "Let's get Mick on the way out."

"Mick?" Peter asked.

"That friend we told you about," Pepper explained.

"Oh, right. I've been wanting to meet him."

"Meet who?" Mick was standing beside them, a guarded look on his face as he sized up Peter.

"Mick, Peter here knows where Terry is," Pepper exclaimed. "He's going to take us to him."

"Really?" Mick eyed Peter's expensive clothes dubiously. "*You* know Terry Han?"

"Old friends." Peter smiled expansively and held out his hand to shake hands. "Peter Yang. It's a pleasure."

Mick shook his hand and nodded. "Mickey Soul." He turned his attention back to Amanda and Pepper. "Listen, I got hold of Gabe, and he's going to meet us at Terry's house."

"Do we know how to get there?" Amanda asked.

"It's right around the corner from here." Mick pointed to the next corner. "That street with all the painted balconies, remember?"

"But Terry's not at his house," Peter cut in.

"He's not?"

"He's at a club just down the street."

Mick looked hesitant.

"Look, we don't need Gabe," Amanda said quickly. "Now that we know where Terry is, we can hook up with Gabe later. Every second we stay out in the open like this just puts us in more danger."

"How do I know we can trust this guy?" Mick murmured.

"He goes to our school!" Pepper said indignantly. "Of course we can trust him."

Peter checked his watch and said pointedly, "Do you want me to take you there, or not? I really don't have time to waste."

"Of course we do." Pepper glared angrily at Mick. "Don't mind him." She took Peter's arm and, with a defiant nod of her head, plunged into the crowd. Amanda and Mick scrambled to keep up with them.

"How could you be so rude?" Amanda hissed to Mick as they wove their way through the surging crowd. "Peter Yang is one of the most respected students at Sutter."

Mick shrugged. "Never judge a book by its cover."

"We can trust Peter Yang," Amanda said simply. "Believe me."

He returned her steady gaze for a moment, then nodded. "Okay. It just feels funny, that's all." He grinned and added, "Of course, after all that's happened lately, I'd suspect my own shadow."

Peter and Pepper turned abruptly to the left. Amanda and Mick followed them into a dark, narrow alley. As soon as they left the crowded street, the noise of the celebration vanished and only the muffled sounds of their footsteps could be heard. The silence was eerie. Amanda shuddered unconsciously.

"Just a little farther," Peter called. He pointed to a soft light bulb glowing above a sunken doorway.

"This is a club?" Mick said hesitantly.

"A private club," Peter replied. "There are dozens of them in Chinatown." He touched Pepper's arm lightly. "Don't worry. It's perfectly safe."

He stood to one side and swung the door inward with his arm. Inside was a small hallway painted a garish red with intricate designs covering the walls. Peter motioned to Amanda to step inside. "After you."

"Thank you." Amanda started to step through the door, but froze in her tracks as she saw a flash of gold on Peter's hand. It was a slender gold ring engraved with a snarling tiger's head. The very same ring she had seen on the boy who had attacked Pepper at the playground.

"It's a trap!" Amanda gasped.

Instantly Peter shoved Amanda forward on her knees into the hallway. Before anyone knew what had happened, Peter had kicked Mick squarely in the solar plexus, knocking the wind out of him. Amanda twisted around on the floor to see Mick slumped on the ground, clutching his stomach and gasping horribly for breath. Pepper stood frozen, her eyes huge with fear.

"Run, Pepper," Amanda screamed. "Get help!"

The shout brought Pepper out of her trance. She turned and raced down the alley. Peter started to chase her, but Amanda lunged forward, grabbed him by the ankle, and tripped him. Pepper disappeared around the corner, and Peter cursed loudly in Chinese.

The inner door opened, and several men ran into the hall. Two of them pinned Mick to the ground, while a third held Amanda's arms behind her back. Peter stood up slowly and glared at Amanda.

"Take them inside and tie them up," he ordered curtly. "Then find that girl—now!"

# CHAPTER FOURTEEN

W|ell, we walked right into that one!"

Amanda couldn't see Mick's face, but she could tell by the sound of his voice that he was thoroughly disgusted by what had just happened.

"How was I supposed to know that Peter Yang, of all people, was involved with the Tigers?" Amanda protested hotly. "He was just a nice, smart, well-dressed boy at school who seemed to have a crush on Pepper."

They were sitting back-to-back on the floor of a musty storeroom with their wrists tightly bound together and their feet tied. Wooden shipping crates with labels written in Chinese and English were stacked around them.

"The whole thing smelled like a trap from the start." Mick tussled violently with the knots around his wrists for a moment, then gave up when they didn't budge. "How could I let you talk me into following that guy?"

"Why shouldn't I have trusted him? Peter Yang is one of the most popular students at Sutter Academy. He said he knew where Terry was. And you certainly didn't have a better plan."

"And then to let myself get sucker-punched by that—that *slime ball*!" Mick pounded his feet against the floor in frustration. "Dumb, dumb, *dumb*!"

"Mick?"

"What?" he snapped.

"Are you finished?"

She felt his back stiffen against hers.

"Because complaining isn't going to get us out of here any sooner." Her voice quivered in her throat. "And now they're after Pepper. She's all alone out there. I wish we could get out of here to help her!"

There was a tense moment of silence. Finally Mick said, "You're right. Let's check the place out and see what we've got to work with. What do you see from your angle?"

Amanda looked carefully around the room. "Aside from a lot of packing crates, not much. There's a pile of old newspapers just to the left of my feet. There's a sliding door at the far end of the room, but it's bolted tight."

Mick nodded. "That should lead to the loading dock on the alley. Anything else? Tools lying around? Crowbars?"

"No."

"Okay. From this end I've got a clean look at the door. It's only got one lock, but it looks like a dead bolt. There's a glass transom over it. That's where our light's coming from." He tilted his head and stared at the ceiling. "No skylights. No heating vents. Nothing."

"How soon do you think they'll be back?"

"As soon as they find Pepper," Mick replied. "Let's hope she remembered how to get to Terry's house."

"I just can't understand why her pictures could have caused such a stir," Amanda said. "Who would go to such trouble to cover up a signal for a drug drop?"

"These guys deal in drugs in a major way," Mick replied. "It could be worth millions of dollars to their syndicate. People have been killed for a lot less."

Something skittered across Amanda's line of vision between the stacks of crates, and her heart leaped into her throat. "What was that?"

"A rat, probably. These old warehouses are crawling with them."

"A *rat?*" Amanda tried to quell the panic rising in her throat. She leaned closer to Mick's back.

"Stop squirming around so much," he said. "I'm trying to work on these knots."

"I'm cold," she replied. "It's damp in here, in case you haven't noticed."

"Pull some of those newspapers around you with your feet," Mick advised. "They're a natural insulator."

Amanda caught the issues on top of the pile with her heels and dragged them close beside her. In a few moments she was snug in a nest of paper. "You're right, it works."

Mick didn't reply, but Amanda could feel his fingers tugging at the knots that bound them. Glancing down at the newspapers, Amanda saw something that made her heart stop.

"Mick?"

"Yeah?"

"Look at this headline."

"Mandy, this is no time to be reading the stupid newspaper."

"No, I'm serious. Look at this."

He craned his neck until he could see the yellowing newspaper lying on the floor beside them. "Chinatown Mobster Arrested for Murder," Mick read out loud. "The San Francisco Police Department today brought charges of conspiracy to commit murder against organized crime kingpin Willie 'the Chairman' Chow." He broke off reading and said, "Yeah, so what? We already know about that."

"Mick, look closer," Amanda urged excitedly.

Mick kept reading. "When Chinatown business leader Lester Fong was found dead in front of his house on Waverly Place at one A.M. on October twenty-ninth . . ."

Amanda heard an intake of breath, then a soft whistle. "This is incredible," Mick said. "That's the same time, the same date—"

"The same location that we found in Pepper's

pictures," Amanda finished gravely. "Keep reading!"

Mick cleared his throat. ". . . police suspected that Mr. Chow had ordered the execution-style murder, but they lacked direct evidence to prove it. Now police have uncovered a witness who has agreed to testify against the Chairman in court—"

"That's the guy who disappeared so suddenly," Amanda interrupted.

"Right. And with him went the case against the Chairman. No evidence."

"Except . . . for Pepper's pictures," Amanda finished in a rush as the truth hit her.

"No wonder they've been after us," Mick said. "That last picture must have something that links the hit directly to the Chairman."

"You mean like his signature?" Amanda asked. Mick nodded. "Wow. I bet they never dreamed anyone would notice a graffiti message scrawled on four different walls."

"And that last piece of the puzzle is locked up at the printer's," Mick added grimly.

They sat quietly for a moment.

"Mick, this is worse than we thought."

"I know. These guys will stop at nothing to get what they want. Even murder. And we're stuck here like a pair of sitting ducks."

The two of them sat in a dull silence. Amanda listened to the rustling behind the packing crates and was overwhelmed with hopelessness. She realized that she might be spending her last moments alive trapped in a gruesome warehouse with hideous rats crawling all around her. It was almost too terrible to think about.

"Mick!" she suddenly blurted. "I never dreamed it would come to this. It all seemed so exciting, trying to figure out the puzzle and solve the mystery, but now . . ." Amanda could feel a tightening in her throat as she fought back her tears. "Mick, there's something I've just got to say."

She could feel his body shift as he listened to her confession.

"I know I'm really stubborn and not the easiest person to get along with. I've said some awful things to you at times . . ." Amanda hesitated for a moment. "What I mean is, I think I've always thought you were wonderful, and having you as a friend means everything to me."

"Me too," Mick answered gruffly. He felt for her hand and clasped it in his.

Amanda felt a surge of warmth at the touch. "I've never met a boy like you," she went on. "I just wish we could have gotten closer, and now there's no time left." Her eyes filled with tears, and she leaned her head back against his.

"I know." Mick spoke in almost a whisper. "Feelings like this happen once in a lifetime, and I . . . I just want to say . . ." He cleared his throat awkwardly.

"Yes?" Amanda could feel her heart pounding

in her chest. For a moment she imagined that she could feel Mick's heart beating, too.

"Mandy, I, uh . . ."

"What is it, Mick?" Amanda encouraged.

Another endless silence passed.

"I . . ." His voice grew suddenly stronger. "I think I've figured a way out of here!"

"Wha—?"

"Listen carefully. You see that nail sticking out of that post?"

Amanda turned and looked in the direction he was indicating. About ten feet away was a heavy post with several nails hammered into it. One of them had been driven completely through the wood, and its sharp point protruded from the other side.

"If we can work our way over to it," Mick explained, "we can cut these ropes with the point."

"How're we going to get over there?"

"When I count to three, press hard against my back with your legs. Maybe we can stand up and hop over to it. Ready? One, two—*three!*"

Amanda dug her feet into the ground and pushed her back into Mick's for all she was worth. The force of her movement knocked them over onto their sides.

"Not so hard!" he shouted. "This move requires balance, not muscle."

Amanda stuck out her tongue. "Well, you said push hard."

Mick chuckled softly. "I didn't realize you were so strong, Now, let's get back to an upright position and try again."

After a lot of grunting and groaning, they finally managed to get back to a sitting position.

"Let's try it again," Mick said. "And go *easy*."

This time when Amanda pressed against his back, she felt his weight balance hers, and they rose surely and smoothly to their feet.

"Now, on the count of two, hop to your left," Mick instructed. "Ready?"

They bumped awkwardly across the floor at first, but finally found a smooth rhythm and reached the post without losing their balance.

"I guess this is what it would feel like to be a Siamese twin," Amanda cracked.

"No kidding," Mick agreed. His voice took on a husky tone. "You know, we make a good team, Hart."

Amanda felt a warm glow at the compliment. "Thanks, Soul."

"Once you remember to follow instructions, that is."

Amanda dug her elbow into his side hard, and Mick groaned. "What'd you do that for?"

"I slipped," Amanda replied innocently. "Now, how do we get down to the nail?"

"Huh? Oh. The same way we got up."

They maneuvered themselves back down to the floor alongside the post, and Mick felt with his fingers for the tip of the nail. "We've got to get in closer."

"How much?" Amanda asked.

"I don't know. I can't see what I'm looking for—*ouch!*"

"Mick?"

There was a short pause. "I found the nail," Mick announced dryly.

Amanda smiled. "Hurry up and cut the ropes."

She could hear a rhythmic chafing as Mick scraped the cord across the point of the nail. After a few minutes there was a snapping sound, and their arms pulled apart. Amanda rubbed her sore wrists gratefully, then pulled with her fingers at the knots binding her feet. By the time she had unraveled them, Mick was already up and checking out the door.

"What do you think?" Amanda said, coming up beside him.

"Like I thought," Mick replied. "Locked tight as a drum."

Amanda took a deep breath, forcing herself to stay calm. "So how do we get out of here?"

Mick smiled and pointed to the transom above the door. There was a single latch keeping the window shut. "We're flying the friendly skies. Help me lug some of these crates over to the door."

"Mick." Amanda pulled at his sleeve. "What if there's a guard posted outside?"

Mick hesitated. "That's just a chance we're going to have to take."

It took only a few moments to stack some empty crates beneath the transom. Mick and Amanda were clambering up toward the light and freedom when a clicking in the lock made them freeze. There was a loud snap as the dead bolt was drawn clear on the other side. Their eyes met for a fleeting moment.

"Mick!" Amanda whispered.

The handle turned in the door. Soundlessly Mick leaped down and set himself between Amanda and the enemy outside.

# CHAPTER FIFTEEN

T he door swung open, and a massive figure stepped into the room. When he saw Mick poised ready to deck him, the figure said in a calm voice, "Whoa."

Mick stopped in midswing. "Gabe?"

Gabe stepped into the light and grinned. "You expecting someone else?"

"Gabe?" Mick leaped forward and wrapped his arms around the enormous teen. "I've never been so happy to see your lousy face in my entire life."

Another figure appeared behind Gabe.

"Terry," Mick exclaimed as he recognized the other boy's wiry frame. "All right!" Mick and Terry gave each other a high five.

Amanda scrambled down from her perch on the crates. "I can't tell you how glad we are to see you two."

"How'd you know where to find us?" Mick asked.

"Once Gabe got to my house, we waited for you to show up," Terry explained.

"But we got impatient," Gabe said. "So we came looking for you."

"Then we ran into some of my old Tiger friends, and Gabe, uh, *persuaded* them to tell us where you were." Terry pointed with a grin to the bruise forming under one of Gabe's eyes.

"I'm a very persuasive guy sometimes," Gabe said with a shrug.

"Where's Pepper?" Amanda asked.

Gabe and Terry looked at her in confusion. "Isn't she with you?"

"No." Amanda's eyes widened with alarm. "She's still out there, Mick. She never made it to Terry's house."

Mick squeezed her hand. "Maybe she made it to the cops."

Just then they heard a familiar voice bellowing from the loading dock outside. "Let go of me, you creeps!"

"Pepper!" Amanda gasped. "They've caught her."

"And they're bringing her back here," Mick whispered.

"What should we do?" Gabe asked.

"Quick—hide behind the crates," Mick ordered. "Mandy and I will act like we're still tied up. Maybe we can catch them off guard."

Terry shut the door while Gabe rewrapped the cords around their wrists and legs.

"Not too tight," Mick warned. "I want to be able to move when I have to."

"Gabe, come on," Terry hissed. "They'll be here any second."

Gabe nodded, and the two boys melted into the shadows at the rear of the warehouse, leaving Mick and Amanda alone. Amanda felt as if her heart were going to leap out of her body, it was pounding so hard.

"Mick?"

"Yeah?" he whispered hoarsely.

"I'm so frightened!"

"So am I."

The sound of the struggle outside intensified as the thugs unlocked the sliding door.

"You take your hands off me," Amanda heard Pepper shout. "My uncle's a federal judge. When I show him those pictures, he'll have you put so far away, you'll forget you ever existed."

"Shut her up," a low voice snapped.

"And another thing—mmmph! Mmmph!"

"That's better," Peter Yang's voice said. "Let's get her inside."

A loud thunk was heard, and a male voice howled with pain. "Don't think you can shut me up that easily!" Pepper roared with renewed intensity.

*Good for you, Pepper,* Amanda thought.

"What's the matter with you guys?" Peter Yang's voice snarled angrily. "Can't you control her? She's just a stupid girl. Put a gag on her."

"She's an alley cat," one of the others complained. "She almost kicked my knee off."

The door slid open, and two men stumbled into
the warehouse, dragging a kicking and struggling
Pepper with them. Peter Yang followed and
quickly locked the door behind them.

A rag had been stuffed into Pepper's mouth.
She fought like a fury until she Amanda and Mick
sitting quietly on the floor. The sight of them
bound drained the fight right out of her, and she
didn't resist as the thugs tied her to a water pipe.

"Man, you blew it," one of the gang members
hissed at Peter. He was a pug-nosed boy with a
squat, thick body. "Those pictures are still out
there, and you'd better do something about it."

Peter Yang, as courtly as ever in his sport coat
and slacks, gave the hood a withering look. "Since
when do you start giving me orders, Eddie?"

"Since you start letting girls outsmart you,
Four-two-six," Eddie retorted.

Amanda gasped. She whispered under her
breath to Mick, "The number on the wall. That's
Peter!"

Peter pulled an ivory money clip out of his
pocket and turned it over and over in his hand as
he talked. "Those pictures are inconsequential."
He pointed to his three prisoners. "We have
them."

"What do you mean?" a taller boy demanded,
stepping forward. "If those pictures get into
court, it'll be all over for the Chairman."

"And us," Eddie grumbled.

"Ah." Peter raised one finger. "You said *if* they

get into court. And that's not going to happen. We're going to make sure of that."

"What do you mean?" Eddie asked.

"Tomorrow morning the Chairman's lawyers will present a motion for dismissal on the grounds of lack of evidence. No incriminating pictures, no new evidence—and Mr. Chow is a free man."

"But what do we do about them, Four-two-six?" The tall boy pointed to Mick, Amanda, and Pepper. "They know all about the messages on the walls."

Peter nodded. "And that's very unfortunate." He stood over Pepper with a contemptuous sneer on his lips. "When you showed me the photos you intended to enter in the competition, I'll admit I was startled. At first I thought, Who would ever make the connection? But it was too risky. So I had your entry removed and destroyed."

Pepper stared up at him, her eyes wide with horror.

"The negatives remained a problem, but I thought you'd be reasonable and give up. You and your friends persisted in meddling, though."

He clucked his tongue disapprovingly.

"If you had just heeded my warning, none of this would have happened. No further measures would have been necessary. As it is . . ."

Peter shrugged and pressed a button on his money clip. The clip was immediately transformed into a gleaming switchblade.

Pepper moaned, and Amanda dug her nails into Mick's hand.

"Here, Eddie." Peter threw the open blade at the feet of the thug. It stuck in the floor inches in front of him. "You're so anxious to do something. Dispose of them. I'll be outside."

Peter turned just as Eddie bent down for the knife. Amanda felt Mick tense beside her and braced herself. It was now or never.

Mick sprang like a cat toward the bent figure. Eddie looked up in surprise just as Mick's fist hit him square in the jaw. He crumpled up like an accordion. Amanda raced to Pepper and untied her with shaking hands.

Peter Yang spun around in shock. Then he lowered himself into a martial arts stance and hissed, "Leave him alone!" As he closed in on Mick, he smiled cruelly. "This will be a pleasure."

Just then Terry Han came flying out of the shadows in a blur of feet and fists. Within moments Peter lay senseless on the ground. "The pleasure was all mine," Terry muttered.

With a roar Gabe charged out of the darkness at the other boy. He jumped up and, grasping a low beam, kicked at the boy's head. The boy fell to the floor, groaning with pain. In a flash, Amanda and Pepper leaped on him and tied his hands behind his back. Terry and Gabe did the same to Eddie and Peter Yang.

"Let's block the door from the outside," Mick commanded. "And then get the hell out of here."

Gabe grabbed the heaviest crate he could find and, once they were outside, wedged it against the door. Then they made their way down the alley and ran for the lights of the street.

The New Year's parade was in full swing. Revelers were streaming by the entrance to the alley in an unbroken chain of bodies. The sound of horns, firecrackers, and gongs was deafening.

"That blockade will hold them only for a little while," Mick shouted to the others over the din. "We need to get into that printer's shop and then to the police as soon as possible. But how are we going to get out of Chinatown?"

Gabe shrugged. "The gangs are everywhere. We'll have to fight our way out."

"Come on, Gabe," Pepper shouted. "That's fine for you to say, but where does that leave Amanda and me?"

"What choice do you have?" Terry yelled back. "We can't sneak out. You Anglos stick out like sore thumbs."

They were still arguing when Amanda noticed a group of young Chinese boys carrying an ornate dragon mask and its long silk body down the alley.

"Wait a minute, boys," Amanda yelled. "Are you taking that dragon costume home now?"

The boy holding the dragon's head looked back and nodded solemnly.

"How would you like to make some quick money?"

The boy looked at the others and shrugged. "Depends on what you want."

"I want to borrow that dragon costume for fifteen minutes," Amanda said.

The boy shook his head violently.

"I'll give you ten dollars. And you can come with us."

He shook his head again.

"Twenty."

He looked at the others hesitantly.

"Twenty-five. And that's my final offer."

The boy grinned and held out the dragon head.

"Amanda, what are you doing?" Mick asked incredulously, as Amanda dug in her pocket for the money. She motioned him to be quiet. After she had paid the boys Amanda instructed Pepper to join her under the costume.

"What do you think?" Amanda called from under the red-and-green silk. "Do we look like Anglos now?"

Mick peeked under the material. "Mandy, you're a genius." He gestured for Gabe and Terry to get under the dragon, too.

Mick took the position at the front, and the others fell in line behind him. As they wove their way down the main street of Chinatown, Amanda was certain she could hear Mick humming "I Love a Parade."

# CHAPTER SIXTEEN

I was almost midnight when they arrived at Pickwick Printers. Pepper's car was still parked around the corner, and Mick opened the trunk. "We need a crow bar, or tire iron, or something."

"What for?" Amanda asked.

Mick blinked at her in amazement. "To break into that building."

"You can't do that. It's illegal."

Mick ran one hand through his hair. "I can't believe you. We've been nearly killed several times this evening, and for all we know, it's not over yet. The one thing that we really need is in this building. What do you suggest we do? Camp out till morning?"

Amanda folded her arms stubbornly. "I think we should call Sergeant Rubano. He'll let us in, and we won't have to break the law."

Pepper glanced nervously over her shoulder. "Well, whatever you do, do it fast so we can get out of here."

A pay phone was located at the edge of the

little white building, and Amanda stepped inside and dialed.

"Precinct headquarters, Sergeant Alverson speaking," a gruff voice answered.

"May I speak to Sergeant Rubano, please?" she asked. "This is an emergency."

"Rubano's home asleep. What can I help you with?"

Amanda hesitated for only a second and then blurted out the story. She was too excited to explain it all properly, so she just cut to the important parts. She told the sergeant about how Pepper's pictures had been stolen and her house broken into.

"Then we thought it might be something in the photos, and Terry's grandmother translated the message for us—and we were right! But before we could do anything, we got caught in a trap and put in a warehouse with rats. Luckily, Gabe and Terry got us out. Then we escaped right under their noses by parading through Chinatown in a dragon costume."

She took a deep breath and finished, "Now we're at the printer's, and the photo is inside, and if you don't hurry and get here, I'm afraid the gang might get us first."

There was a long silence at the other end of the line. "Now, run that by me again. You say your friend took some pictures for the school paper?"

"No!" Amanda shouted in frustration. "Look, Officer, I don't have time to go over this all again.

A Chinatown gang is after us, and what I want to know is—are you going to help us or not?"

"What is this?" the policeman demanded. "A practical joke?"

Amanda realized that he thought she was making it all up. She looked over at Mick, who stood by the window clutching a tire iron. She sighed and then announced loudly, so her friends on the street could hear, "This is no joke. I want to report a robbery in progress at Pickwick Printers."

As she gave the address, Mick grinned and smashed the window with the tire iron. Then Gabe carefully reached his arm through the shattered glass and unlocked the door.

The alarm went off with a shrill blast. Amanda hung up the phone and leaned against the wall. "I guess he believes me now."

The next morning, five exhausted teens waited outside the courtroom in City Hall. They were still wearing the same clothes from the night before. Their eyes were slightly red from lack of sleep, but they were happy.

"I'm glad they finally reached Sergeant Rubano," Amanda declared.

"Yeah, it was worth spending the night at the police station just to have him apologize in person," Mick said with a grin.

Amanda laughed. "He not only apologized—he said he plans on getting us the key to the city."

"If you'd spent five years trying to nail the Chairman," Gabe cracked, "you'd be happy, too."

There had been only one damper on the whole event. As the three of them had entered City Hall that morning, they had passed by the Picture the City exhibition. First prize had been awarded to Richard Reely.

"Pep?" Amanda asked, joining her friend at the water cooler. "Do you feel awful that you didn't win the photo contest?"

Pepper took a sip of her water and then crumpled her cup and tossed it in the trash can. "Why should I feel bad? I may not have won the fortune, but I certainly got the fame."

She pointed to a huge blowup of her final photograph leaning against the wall beside enlargements of the other three. Several guards watched over them carefully. The Chinese character in the bottom of the final shot clearly revealed the signature of the Chairman.

"The only thing I feel bad about is Peter. I mean, how could I have such lousy taste in men?"

"Don't feel bad." Amanda looped her arm over Pepper's shoulder. "He fooled everyone."

Mick shrugged. "Hey, Peter was a leader, no matter how you look at it."

"That's true," Terry Han agreed. "He wasn't just a lowly gang member. He was a four-two-six."

Amanda looked up curiously. "By the way—what *is* a four-two-six?"

The three boys exchanged looks. Then Terry answered softly, "Four-two-six is the code number given by the gangs to the person who is their executioner."

Pepper gasped. "You mean, a hit man?"

Mick nodded. "Peter's other code name was the Mongoose. They kill snakes."

Amanda snapped her fingers. "Now I get it— so the message that Pepper photographed was an order from Chow, the Chairman, ordering Peter, the Mongoose, to execute Mr. Fong, the Big Snake."

Mick nodded. "Fong had been leading a movement to wipe out the gangs, so the Chairman had Peter kill him."

"On October twenty-ninth at one A.M.," Gabe added.

"At Waverly Place," Terry finished.

Mick made a sweeping gesture to Pepper's photographs. "The evidence is all there in black and white."

"But he's so young," Amanda murmured in shock.

"Peter Yang was born into crime," Terry Han said. "We found out that Willie Chow is his uncle."

"What?" Amanda gasped.

"But how could he be part of a gang?" Pepper asked. "He was in school with us every day."

"Peter Yang led two separate lives," Mick explained. "During the day, he was the model student. After school, he worked for his uncle." He laughed thinly. "Some part-time job."

"You mean he actually *killed* people?" Amanda asked with an involuntary shudder.

"Rubano thinks he had his thugs do it for him," Terry said. "But Peter planned the murders, and he took the credit for them in the organization."

"The Chairman was grooming Peter to take over his gang when he got too old," Gabe added.

"They called him the rising star of the underworld." Mick shook his head in amazement. "Peter Yang would have been the perfect criminal—a respectable businessman on the outside, and a ruthless killer underneath. And no one would have ever known."

All of a sudden Pepper looked very ill. "I can't believe I had a crush on a murderer. I think I'm going to faint."

Gabe caught her by the arm and led her to a nearby bench. "*Chica,* you can't give in now—you have to testify."

As if in answer to Gabe's words, a deputy stuck her head into the hall from the courtroom. "Miss Larson? You're next."

Amanda hugged Pepper. "Are you scared?"

"Who, me, scared?" Pepper shoved her glasses up on her nose. "I'm absolutely petrified."

As two guards carried in the photo exhibit, Gabe helped Pepper to her feet. "Come on," he said gently. "I'll go with you."

Mick and Amanda watched them enter the courtroom, and then Amanda turned to Mick.

"Um, Mick?" Amanda asked hesitantly. "When we were tied together last night, and I was sure we were going to die . . ."

Mick nodded.

"Well, I said some pretty emotional things. But I was under a lot of stress, and—"

Mick put his finger to her lips. "Mandy, you don't have to apologize. I understand."

She blushed and stared down at the floor. Then Mick took both of her hands in his and murmured, "You know, last night, when I started to say something, too, but didn't get the chance?"

Amanda tilted her chin up to look into his clear blue eyes. "Yes?"

"Well, I meant every word of it."

She blinked at him uncomprehendingly. But before she could say another word Mick's lips met hers. It was a soft, tender kiss that made her forget about the gangs and drug wars, and their close brush with death. All she could think about was making this kiss last forever.

## ABOUT THE AUTHOR

JAHNNA N. MALCOLM is really the pen name for a husband-and-wife team, Jahnna Beecham and Malcolm Hillgartner. Together they have written twenty-one books, including five titles for Bantam's Sweet Dreams series under the name Jahnna Beecham. They are also the authors of a middle-grade series called Bad News Ballet. Both are professional actors and have trod the boards in theaters across the United States and Europe. In fact, they met in an audition and were married on the stage. Jahnna and Malcolm live in Montana with their brand-new baby Dashiell and two old dogs.

# All-Star Movie and TV Favorites
## *The Hottest Teen Heartthrobs!*

These terrific star bios are packed with the juicy details *you* want to know.  Here's the inside scoop on the star's family life, friends, tips on dating, life on the set, future career plans, *plus* fantastic photo inserts.

☐ **ALYSSA MILANO:** SHE'S THE BOSS by Grace Catalano     28158 $2.75

☐ **RIVER PHOENIX:** HERO AND HEARTTHROB by Grace Catalano     27728 $2.75

☐ **KIRK CAMERON:** DREAM GUY by Grace Catalano     27135 $2.75

## From the World of Rock!

☐ **DEBBIE GIBSON:** ELECTRIC STAR by Randi Reisfeld     28379 $2.95

☐ **NEW KIDS ON THE BLOCK** by Grace Catalano     28587 $3.50

## ☆ *Plus...don't miss exciting movie and TV tie-ins of these top favorites!*

☐ **DEAD POETS SOCIETY** by N.H. Kleinbaum     28298 $2.95

☐ **HEAD OF THE CLASS** by Susan Beth Pfeffer     28190 $2.95